FELIX'S NEW VENTURE

"I'll take care of you, Blackie. You'll never have to leave King Farm."

Alec stopped and listened, unnoticed, watching through a crack in the wood of the stall. Felix was brushing Blackie to as much of a sheen as is possible with an old workhorse. He spoke to the animal in a low, soothing voice.

"No more out to pasture for you. You still got a lot of good years left. Yes sir! Now stand still, there's a good boy. I'll bet you haven't had a grooming like this for a long time. But you have to look good. We have some deliveries to make this morning. Here, I've got a reward for you."

Alec shook his head slowly and smiled as Felix took an apple out of his pocket and sank his teeth into one side of it. Blackie took a big bite out of the other side of the apple, taking it right from the boy's mouth. Felix giggled as the horse's muzzle tickled him.

**Also available in the Road to Avonlea Series
from Bantam Skylark books**

Felix and Blackie

Storybook written by

Heather Conkie

Based on the Sullivan Films Production
written by Heather Conkie
adapted from the novels of

Lucy Maud Montgomery

A BANTAM SKYLARK BOOK®
NEW YORK · TORONTO · LONDON · SYDNEY · AUCKLAND

Based on the Sullivan Films Production produced by Sullivan Films Inc.
in association with CBC and the Disney Channel with the participation
of Telefilm Canada adapted from Lucy Maud Montgomery's novels.

Teleplay written by Heather Conkie
Copyright © 1991 by Sullivan Films Distribution, Inc.

This edition contains the complete text
of the original edition.
NOT ONE WORD HAS BEEN OMITTED.

RL 6, 008–012

FELIX AND BLACKIE
A Bantam Skylark Book / published by arrangement with
HarperCollins Publishers Ltd.

PUBLISHING HISTORY
HarperCollins edition published 1994
Bantam edition / May 1994

ROAD TO AVONLEA is the trademark of Sullivan Films Inc.

Skylark Books is a registered trademark of Bantam Books,
a division of Bantam Doubleday Dell Publishing Group, Inc.
Registered in U.S. Patent and Trademark Office and elsewhere.

ISBN 0-553-48121-5

Bantam Books are published by Bantam Books, a division of Bantam Doubleday Dell
Publishing Group, Inc. Its trademark, consisting of the words "Bantam Books" and the
portrayal of a rooster, is Registered in U.S. Patent and Trademark Office and in other
countries. Marca Registrada. Bantam Books, 1540 Broadway, New York, New York 10036.

PRINTED IN THE UNITED STATES OF AMERICA
OPM   0   9   8   7   6   5   4   3   2   1

Chapter One

Felix King gripped the side of the buggy as it bounced and swayed in the ruts. A sudden deluge of rain had swept over the island during the night and had eroded parts of the red gravel road, making the going a little rougher than usual. The huge black horse seemed to be deliberately pulling the wagon through the deepest potholes he could find, and eleven-year-old Felix felt his jaw gingerly, positive that his teeth were looser than they had been when he and his father set out from the King farm to the general store. He smiled to himself as he looked at the horse's enormous back and shoulders, swaying rhythmically. *Blackie probably just wanted to make sure we were awake*, he thought.

Felix threw his head back and looked up at the sky. It was cobalt blue with just a few white, fluffy clouds scudding across. The night's storm had headed east towards the mainland, and the morning had dawned chilly and bright. Felix was suddenly glad his mother had made him put on an extra sweater. Not that he would ever admit that to her, of course.

Abruptly, the blue sky gave way to complete darkness, and Blackie's hooves echoed hollowly on the boards of the covered bridge until his passengers emerged, blinking, into the bright sunlight once again. The village of Avonlea lay before them, nestled comfortably against a background of fields and forest. The brilliant red and copper leaves of the trees waved in the wind like flags in the crisp autumn light, blazing against the rich green of the pines.

Alec King pulled on the reins lightly, but the big black horse had followed the route into the village so many times that he knew the way automatically. He slowed his pace and came to a halt in front of the general store hitching post, almost out of pure habit.

The bushels of fruits and vegetables covering the store's front porch rivaled the colors of the autumn trees. Amber-gold acorn squash and bright-orange pumpkins were stacked high beside creamy potatoes and baskets full of deep-red russet apples.

Lean and tanned from the hard work that follows any harvest, Alec jumped down from the buggy and called to his son as he entered the general store. "Stay with Blackie, Felix. I won't be long."

Felix frowned and threw his cap onto the floor of the buggy. He pushed his brown hair out of his eyes and whistled a vague little tune. He wished he could go into the store with his father. He had his heart set on a pair of skates that were just his size, if he wore a couple of extra pairs of socks inside them. His father had noticed him eyeing them the last time they were in town and had told him to save up his money. Pretty hard to do on the allowance he got, Felix thought ruefully to himself.

Felix had tried to save, in good faith. His frown deepened, and he pulled his cap back onto his head and over his eyes. Why had he lost all his savings on that bet with Rupert Gillis? He should have known the bigger boy could take him at arm wrestling. He had lasted fifty whole seconds, though, he reminded himself. That was better than the last time.

Blackie was munching contentedly on a few sparse blades of grass when Felix sighed with exaggerated boredom and jumped down from the buggy. He patted the horse's neck affectionately and glanced down the street. Instantly, he spotted his cousin, Sara Stanley, hanging around outside the post office. Just the person he wanted to see! He and his cousin had shared many adventures together and were quite close—when they weren't fighting. Giving Blackie one last pat, Felix wandered over.

"Hey! Sara! What'cha doin'?" sang out Felix as he approached the blond-haired, blue-eyed girl, who sat with her chin in her hands on the doorstep of the Avonlea post office.

Sara, as always, was beautifully dressed. Her well-cut gray wool coat was trimmed with a black velvet collar and cuffs. Her hat had a matching black velvet ribbon around its brim. Her Nanny Louisa had sent it to her from Paris, a fact that, Felix knew very well, made his sister Felicity as jealous as a cat.

Sara looked up at Felix and smiled. "I'm waiting for Aunt Hetty. She's in there," she motioned to the door.

Felix stuck his hands in his pockets and made a circle in the gravel with his toe. "Uh, Sara, you wouldn't happen to know what Aunt Hetty has planned for the big mathematics test next week, would you?"

Sara looked at him in righteous astonishment. "No! Why would I?"

"Well, she must keep a copy of it at Rose Cottage. With the answers maybe...?" Felix's voice trailed off.

Sara was amazed at her cousin's audacity. Leaping to her feet, she looked him fiercely in the eye, her face a picture of wounded sensibilities.

"Felix King! Do you think that I would stoop so low as to go through Aunt Hetty's papers just for a stupid test?"

Felix frowned and pursed his lips. He had no doubt that *he* would be capable of stooping that low.

"Well..." he muttered, "I just thought..."

Sara plopped herself down on the step once again and returned her chin to the cup of her hands. "Besides," she added, "she keeps it locked up at the schoolhouse."

Felix grinned. That was more like the Sara he knew.

"If you'd just study instead of looking for an easy way out, maybe you wouldn't need to cheat!" his twelve-year-old cousin admonished.

"I don't!" protested Felix. Why did all girls sound the same, even when they grew up to be as old as his mother? He was about to say just that to

Sara when he noticed that she was staring bug-eyed in the direction of the general store.

"Felix! Look!" she yelled.

Felix followed her gaze. Blackie's head had disappeared—into one of the barrels of fresh apples.

"Oh no!" Felix groaned, and both he and Sara took off down the street at a gallop, calling to the horse.

"Blackie! No!"

Without anyone to keep his head firmly held by the reins, the old horse had immediately found his favorite snack and was in the process of devouring it. By the time Felix pulled the huge animal away, the beast had consumed half the apples in the barrel. Sara hastily took a few apples from the top of the pile that had obviously been nibbled and held them behind her back.

As luck would have it, Mrs. Lawson chose that moment to come out of the store with Alec King.

Felix and Sara stood in wide-eyed innocence by the guilty animal, who continued to chomp contentedly, telltale pieces of apple falling from his mouth.

"Hello, Uncle Alec," chirped Sara, hoping to divert the attention of the grown-ups somewhat, but with no success.

Mrs. Lawson's usual good-humored smile froze. Pursing her lips, she reached into the almost empty barrel and picked out an apple. She turned it gingerly in her fingers and looked down her nose at it in disgust. It was completely covered in teeth marks. She glanced severely from Sara to Felix, her eyes finally resting on an unconcerned Blackie. She took a deep breath, and then, without a word, Mrs. Lawson gave them all one last withering look and returned inside the store with a swish of her skirt. Blackie watched her go, and swished his tail in a like manner.

Alec shook his head and looked heavenward. "I told you to stay with the horse, Felix!"

Sara felt the time to leave had come. "I'd better be going!" she said cheerily. "I have to meet Aunt Hetty!" She turned on her heel and ran towards the post office.

Alec was about to say more to his son when Abner Jeffries hurried across the street from the blacksmith's shop, wiping his hands on the front of his leather apron.

"Alec King! How are you today?" called Abner in a suitably commanding voice. When he wasn't working as a blacksmith, Abner was the Chief Constable of Avonlea, and so impressed was he by this lofty appointed position that he often spoke in an extremely pompous and puffed-up manner.

Alec gave Felix one more warning look that

said, in no uncertain terms, "This time, stay with the horse" and walked to meet Abner, his hand stretched out in greeting.

"You're just the fellow I wanted to talk to!" boomed the Chief Constable. "You still looking for a horse?"

Alec took Abner's arm and quickly drew him further away from Felix.

"Well...I'm still thinking about it..." he mumbled, putting a finger to his lips, hoping the man would take a hint and not speak quite so loudly in front of his son.

"Well," Abner continued, in a more conspiratorial tone, "if you're interested at all, I heard of one for sale at the racetrack over in Summerside! If you're still in the market, that is."

Alec was about to interject, but Abner pushed on.

"You'll have to have a look at it today, though, not tomorrow, because I understand the owner, Pat Shore, is leaving for Halifax right soon...and he has to sell! From what I hear, it's the deal of a lifetime!"

Alec looked over his shoulder to where Felix was patting Blackie's neck in a comforting manner.

"Well Abner, I can't very well take Felix to a racetrack. Janet would have my hide."

Abner shook his head and wagged his finger simultaneously. "Alec King, I know horseflesh!

There will never be another chance like this!"

Alec smiled. "Well, thanks for the tip, Abner. I'll keep it in mind."

Abner frowned as he tipped his hat and returned to the smithy. It was as plain as day the Chief Constable felt he had wasted his valuable information on an unappreciative audience.

Alec walked back to the buggy deep in thought. Abner Jeffries knew a lot about horses' hooves, but did that make him an expert on horses? On the other hand, maybe it was worth a look. Janet wouldn't need to know.

"C'mon, Felix!" he called. "We've got one more stop to make."

Felix leapt up into the buggy and looked sideways at his father. Whatever Abner had said, he was thankful for it. It had certainly taken the heat off Blackie's little transgression.

Chapter Two

The Summerside racetrack was a beehive of activity as father and son made their way through the lineups of men waiting to place their bets.

"So this is what the track is like!" Felix marvelled as he took a deep breath of air, pungent with the smell of horses and hay. He could barely contain his excitement. He had never been at the track before, and he knew very well it was forbidden territory.

Felix had been spellbound as the powerful animals thundered around the track towards the finish line, urged on by their jockeys and the crowds. His ears still rung with the clamor of the excited racing fans as they cheered for their favorite horses. He and his father had yelled along with the best of them. Especially when, against the odds, the animal of their choice had come in first!

"That Majestic Murphy is some horse!" Felix continued, grinning up at Alec. "What're you gonna do with all the money you won? Wait'll mother finds out!"

Alec cleared his throat. That was something he fervently hoped would never happen. For some reason, Janet had a total aversion to anything to do with betting or gambling. She felt almost as if the money derived from such sport was positively tainted, even if it were put to good use.

Alec remembered the last time he had been lucky with the horses. He had gone out immediately and bought his wife a dress she had been admiring at the general store. He could see it now—blue with a collar made out of some kind of lace. Quite pretty, he had thought, even though he didn't know very much about dresses. Janet had been overjoyed, until Mr. Lawson had let the cat out of the bag by congratulating him heartily on his winnings, right in front of her. A furious Janet immediately took the dress to the church and put it in the poor box.

Alec gave his son a wink. "It might, uh...be best if we don't mention anything about this to your mother. We'll just keep it a secret between us... "

Felix began to protest, but then, suddenly, he understood and winked back, nodding at his father wisely, man to man. "You can count on me."

"Besides," continued Alec, "I didn't come to the track expressly to bet."

Felix shook his head solemnly. "No, no. Of course not."

Alec smiled. "I didn't!" he insisted. "I've heard of a horse that's up for sale, apparently at a very reasonable price. I just want to take a look at it... that's all."

"Of course," agreed Felix reasonably as they pushed through the crowd, now beginning to head for their buggies and home. "Why do we need another horse?" he asked after a short pause.

They made a sharp right turn down an alley between long rows of stalls and found their path blocked by a large horse-drawn cart marked with the sign "Webster's Delivery." Bales of hay were being unloaded. The owner of the rig strode into view and was just about to hoist himself into the driver's seat when he spotted Alec and waved a greeting.

Hank Webster was a big, swarthy, muscular man with curly black hair and twinkling blue eyes that threw you off guard. You never knew whether they were laughing *with* you, or *at* you. Alec had known Hank for years, since they were boys, and the fellow had never changed. He had always been the school bully, prone to swaggering and bragging. Coming from a very poor family, the middle boy of seven children, he'd had to fight for everything. Ever since Alec could remember, Hank had been searching for the almighty dollar. But you had to hand it to him Alec thought, he had certainly made something of himself. "Webster's Delivery" was said to be a very successful business.

"Alec King!" The fellow came forward and, towering over Alec, shook his hand with a hearty and powerful grasp. "Don't see you at the track very often."

Alec tried not to wince. The man's handshake was like a vise grip.

"Hello Hank. Just looking around."

Hank Webster finally let go of his hand and grinned, one gold tooth glinting in the sunlight.

"Is this little Felix?" he boomed, and it was Felix's turn to wince. Little Felix! Who did this fellow think he was, anyway?

"Sure is," mumbled Alec, sensing his son's extreme discomfort.

Hank guffawed and spat on the ground. "Never too young to learn the horses, right Alec?"

Alec smiled ruefully, and any further conversation was thankfully interrupted by the track foreman, anxious to wind up his business transaction with Webster's Delivery service.

Felix's eyes widened as he watched Hank accept a thick roll of bills in payment for the hay delivery. The man licked his finger and flicked through the money, counting it slowly and carefully, making sure his audience had a good long look.

Felix was amazed. He hurried to catch up with his father, who had tired of Hank's exhibition of success and was strolling purposefully towards one of the last stalls in the row.

"Did you see all that money?" marveled Felix. "Boy, I'll bet it was more than you won!"

Alec smiled and pushed his son's cap playfully over his eyes. Trust Felix to be impressed with money. Felix adjusted his cap and followed his father through the crowd.

Pat Shore led a fine-looking stallion out of its stall and patted it on the forehead with affection. The animal was a palomino, with a golden coat and a light-blond mane and tail. It had a white star on its forehead and one distinctive white leg. It looked as if it had lost all its white socks save for one, Felix couldn't help thinking.

The owner, a thin, slightly bent man, wrinkled and aged beyond his years, was certainly not as sleek and well cared for as his animal. His lined face was worn and weathered with a million worries and cares.

"I wouldn't be selling him if I didn't have to," he said quietly to Alec. "But I need the cash. I'm moving to Halifax and I can't afford to take him with me. I've already got eight human mouths to feed."

"He's a pretty good size," remarked Alec as he circled the horse appraisingly.

"Oh, he's a big one all right. But you know, he was quite a racer in his day. Won the provincial derby two years in a row. You'll get your money's worth from Caesar, here."

Pat Shore stroked the animal once again, and it was obvious from the look in his eyes that selling Caesar was not an easy thing for him to do.

"What do you think, Felix?" Alec slapped his son on the back.

Felix circled the horse as his father had done, hands on his hips, and nodded slowly. "Guess he's okay," he mumbled, still puzzled as to why his father felt they needed another horse in the first place.

"That means we'll take him, Mr. Shore."

Alec held out his hand and the man shook it warmly. "I'm glad to know he'll have a good home."

A shadow fell over the stall, and Felix turned to see Hank Webster draped in its opening, taking in the handshake.

"Uh huh," he said, a small smile on his stubbled face. "I see I'm too late."

"I'm afraid so, Hank," replied Alec good-naturedly.

The man chewed thoughtfully on a piece of hay. "I was thinkin' of expandin' a bit, you know? Two wagons, two drivers..."

"I heard your business is thriving," commented Alec.

"Can't complain! I deliver clear 'cross the Island now!" boasted the man loudly, spitting out pieces of hay right across the floor of the stall. "But," he said as he whacked Alec on the back, "first come, first served! You got yourself a real deal, Alec! He's a fine piece of horseflesh." He tipped his cap and backed out of the stall, ignoring Felix entirely. "See ya later, Pat!"

Felix watched as his father peeled some bills from his roll of winnings. Pat Shore accepted the payment and once again wished his horse well. He turned away quickly as Alec led Caesar out of the stall and Felix followed.

Chapter Three

"But, why do we need another horse?" demanded Felix. "We've got Blackie."

Almost as if he had heard his name, Blackie snorted loudly and looked over his massive shoulders with an air of disdain towards the newly acquired Caesar. The stallion cantered along behind them, skittish, pulling at the rope that tied him to the back of the buggy.

"Well," Alec replied, slowly and carefully, "Blackie's getting on you know, Felix..."

"No he's not!" his son protested. "He's the smartest horse alive. Blackie knows every word you say."

Alec sighed. He had known this would not be easy. "Well, smart or not, Blackie's an old horse. I've been thinking of selling him."

Felix was thunderstruck. "Sell him!" he blurted out. "Sell Blackie?"

Once again, with uncanny timing, Blackie whinnied and looked around at them, tossing his mane with contempt.

"You see, he heard you," Felix said reproachfully.

Sell Blackie! It was unthinkable. Blackie wasn't just any old barn animal, he was almost a pet. Blackie had been on the King farm since Felix could remember. In fact, one of his first memories was of his father picking him up and perching him on the gigantic horse's back, holding his hand tightly as Blackie took him gently around the corral. He couldn't have been more than two years old. And the time Blackie had been sick and Felix had spent the entire night in the stall, sleeping beside the huge, gentle animal. And swimming with him every summer in the creek. No one had ever seen a horse who liked the water so much. He felt his eyes smart with tears.

Alec looked sideways at Felix as his son continued in a whisper, "How could you even think such a thing? He's part of the family. Blackie's been around forever!"

"Exactly," said Alec in an undertone, immediately embarrassed because he too had lowered his voice for fear the horse would hear him. "Blackie's old, Felix," he continued firmly. "And soon he'll be too old to be of any use to us at all. It's too expensive to feed a workhorse if it can't do any work."

Felix threw his arms up in dismay. "Oh, that's just fine, isn't it? Would you sell me if I couldn't do my work around the farm?"

Alec chuckled and looked at his outraged son, his eyes twinkling suddenly. "If that was the case, we'd have sold you years ago!"

Felix was in no mood for little jokes, especially ones at his own expense.

"Please father, this isn't funny! We have to keep him!"

"Felix..." Alec tried to get a word in, but his son was getting more worked up by the second.

"Let me have him, then!" he countered. "I'll take care of him!"

"Oh, you will?" said his father, with good-natured sarcasm. "How are you going to pay for his keep?"

Felix frowned and looked at the shiny, solid horse that strode before them, pulling his load with bruised dignity.

"I...don't know. I just will, that's all!"

There had to be a way. The thought of someone, a stranger, coming to the King farm and taking Blackie away was inconceivable. Felix's mouth was set with uncharacteristic determination. Blackie was not going to spend his last years away from the family who loved him.

"I...I...you could hire us...we'd work for you...!" It was a stroke of sheer genius. His father was incredibly fond of the work ethic. It worked every time...well, almost every time.

"Felix, I'm not paying you to do your chores!"

His father's voice was final, and Felix knew there was no point in pursuing that tack. He continued gamely. "Well, maybe someone else will hire us to do theirs! Aunt Hetty...or..."

"Hetty?" snorted his father. "Oh c'mon, Felix!"

Hetty King, Alec's oldest sister, was the last person Felix could expect to earn a wage from. She was notoriously tight with her purse strings and expected that all her nephews and nieces should be more than pleased to run errands for her and do chores free of charge. Indeed, as the schoolmistress of Avonlea, she felt it her due that the entire student body be at her beck and call.

Felix's eyes widened as a penny dropped. Suddenly his mind was clear as a bell.

"I know! Blackie and I could work for Mr. Webster. He said he was gonna expand." Just as quickly another brainstorm of an idea hit him. He couldn't believe he hadn't thought of it immediately. "Wait...a...minute! Better still! I'll start my own delivery service!"

His father sighed. "Felix, you can hardly finish your own chores half the time, let alone handle a job."

Felix was fired up and full of answers. "It would only be part time! I know I can do it! It'd keep Blackie in feed. Please! I want to show you I can do it! I don't want you to sell him!"

Alec could not ignore the tone of Felix's voice. How often had he wished he could hear it more? The sound of ambition, the first signs of self-motivation and inner strength. Felix was one of those boys who put more effort and time into avoiding work than the work would have taken in the first place. How many times a week did he and Janet find themselves scolding Felix about something he had started and not finished? They were always encouraging him to do things all the way...not by halves...to take on responsibility. How could he say no now?

"Well...I'll have to think about it..." Alec said slowly.

Felix was quick to seize his advantage. "You're always saying I should take on more responsibility!" he stated, almost as if he had read his father's mind.

Alec looked at him with affection, seeing his wife's impulsiveness shining in his son's eyes. "You've got your mother's gift of persuasion, my boy."

"Please?" continued Felix, unabating.

"You're ready for more responsibility, are you?"

"Yes! Definitely! Never readier!"

His father paused. "All right...but only—"

Alec didn't have a chance to finish. "Thank you! Thank you!" yelled Felix, almost falling out of the buggy in his enthusiasm.

"Listen to me now!" Alec cautioned. "This is on a trial basis. It mustn't interfere with either your schoolwork or your chores."

"I promise! I won't let you down, Father," Felix said solemnly. "Blackie won't either."

Felix leaned against the back of the seat, feeling the thrill of charting his own destiny for the first time. Blackie looked over at him and gave what Felix considered a small whinny of triumph...and thanks.

Chapter Four

Janet King sighed and pushed a stray strand of honey-colored hair out of her eyes. She tried once again to do up a button on the tiny white under-shirt, but baby Daniel was positively bursting from his clothes, and his constant wriggling was doing nothing to help her progress.

"Daniel," his mother announced, "you are going through another one of those growth spurts Dr. Blair is always talking about! Soon, you'll have outgrown everything!"

Daniel gurgled, looking up at her with huge, dark eyes from the kitchen table where Janet was attempting to dress him. She straightened up and rubbed her back, looking forward to the day when he could dress himself. Daniel started kicking his legs vigorously in the air and she went back to the job at hand, trying to put his waving arms into the sleeves of a red-and-blue sweater.

Felix suddenly burst noisily through the back door into the sunny kitchen ahead of his father.

"Mother! Guess what!" Felix bellowed. "I'm going to start a delivery service, with Blackie!"

Janet smiled. "That's nice, dear," she said absently, distracted by the baby's antics. "Really Daniel! It would be easier to dress a slippery eel."

Felix grabbed some apples and cookies from the sideboard and gathered them into his coat.

"It's going to be my responsibility. I'm gonna earn the money to keep him." He headed to the door, shouting over his shoulder. "I'll unhook Blackie from the buggy, Father. Don't worry. I'll make sure she's safe in the barn."

Janet finished buttoning the baby's sweater and suddenly looked up, comprehending for the first time what Felix had said.

"Felix...?" she managed to sputter as the door slammed with a racket and her oldest boy was gone, on the run.

"Fine, son," said Alec, slightly after the fact. He shook his head, smiling wanly.

"A delivery service!" exclaimed Janet, scooping the baby up from the table. "But Alec, he's only a boy. How can he handle something like that all by himself?"

Alec took Daniel from his wife and swooped him up high into the air, eliciting chuckles of delight from the infant.

"I'll help him get started. It'll be good for him to have a little responsibility...right, Daniel?"

Alec gave Janet a quick kiss and, after handing a laughing Daniel over to her, made his way to the door.

"Oh, by the way," he threw over his shoulder, "I...uh...bought a new horse today...it was a good deal!"

The door closed behind him, leaving Janet once

again speechless with astonishment.

"Horse! A horse!" she cried, as what he had just said began to sink in. "Alec!"

She carried Daniel to the kitchen window and looked out across the yard as father and son walked across the driveway towards the barn, Alec's arm around Felix's shoulders. Felix was leading Blackie, and she supposed the other monster of an animal must be the new acquisition.

Her mood changed from exasperation to pride as she watched, and she found her eyes suddenly clouding with tears. She hugged the baby to her, feeling the dewy softness of his skin on her cheek.

"Oh Daniel. You boys grow up so fast."

A dirty and exasperated Felicity King was busy mucking out one of the stalls in the barn when Felix appeared, leading Blackie proudly. He patted the horse's muzzle and gave him an apple.

Felicity narrowed her eyes and pushed away a glossy brown curl that was plastered to her forehead in the heat. She stomped up behind her younger brother and, with a glare, pushed a rake at him.

"Felix King, it's about time you showed up! Here! This is *your* job! *You* finish it!"

As usual, Felix paid no attention whatsoever to his thirteen-year-old sister. Ignoring her was such a habit that he hardly noticed he was doing it. Besides, he had much more important things to think about.

He and Blackie were going into business—"The Felix King Delivery Service." He could see his fleet of wagons in his mind's eye, painted bright blue with his name shining in gold letters. And not just two rigs like Hank Webster, but half a dozen...maybe even a dozen! He'd put every other delivery service on the Island out of business. He thought about the thick roll of bills he had seen the foreman at the track hand over to Mr. Webster, and suddenly he had a vision of himself in a three-piece pinstriped suit, depositing a heavy bag of his week's earnings at the bank in Summerside. He and Blackie were going to be rich!

"Felix! Do you hear me?" Felicity's voice pierced through his daydream. Scowling at her, he closed Blackie's stall door and walked away.

"Where have you been?" Felicity poked him with the handle of the rake, and her voice echoed shrilly in the silence of the barn. Felix winced slightly. There were times when she was harder to ignore than others. Especially when he knew deep down that she had a right to be angry. The horrible task of raking all the manure out of the stalls was his job, one that he tried to avoid as often as possible. But it wasn't his fault, he reasoned. He hadn't asked to go the track. That had been his father's idea. He was about to tell Felicity exactly why he was late when, just in time, he remembered the promise of silence he had made to his father. If Felicity knew they had gone to Summerside to the races, it would be no time flat before his mother found out.

Once again his sister interrupted his thoughts. "I'm sick of doing your chores as well as my own! Where have you been all day?"

Without answering, Felix crossed to the far side of the barn. He threw a hay-covered tarp off an old wooden cart and stood back to survey its peeling, reddish-brown paint and slightly lopsided appearance. It wasn't exactly the fleet of his dreams, but it had potential.

"What are you doing?" demanded Felicity as her father entered the barn.

Felix pounced on him. "Father! Can I use this?" he demanded. Alec rocked back on his heels and surveyed the broken-down vehicle with grave consideration. "Well, it certainly could do with a fresh coat of paint..."

"But it's perfect," insisted Felix.

Felicity could no longer control her patience or her curiosity. "Perfect for what?" she demanded.

"My delivery service," replied Felix loftily. *That will shut her up*, he thought.

"Your what?" said Felicity, her voice thick with sarcasm.

Alec decided it would be best to stay out of the friction-filled relationship of his two eldest children. They very rarely, if ever, saw eye to eye.

"Well, if you're willing to fix it up, you're welcome to have it," Alec said, and picking up the extra bridle and bit he had come to fetch, he continued on his way.

Felix beamed. "Thank you. You won't be sorry. I can't wait to start!"

"Here!" said Felicity bluntly. "Start on this!" She handed him the rake and stalked off.

"But only after I finish my chores, of course," Felix hurried to say, in response to his father's backward glance.

"Of course," said Alec, and he disappeared out of the barn, bridle in hand.

Chapter Five

"Felix's Delivery." The fancy red lettering on the sign stood out beautifully on the side of the cart. Sara stood back, paintbrush in hand, to admire her work. The previously dilapidated wagon had been turned into a thing of beauty. She and Felix had spent days repairing and sanding it. One of the wheels had had to be replaced, and a brand-new driver's seat had been installed. And yesterday, the biggest transformation of all had taken place! Two coats of cornflower-blue paint had been applied.

Sara smiled. She thought she had never seen anything more delightful in her life. Baby Daniel must have agreed, because he sat in his carriage and clapped his hands in glee at the sight of it.

Felix came out of the barn leading Blackie and whistled in appreciation when he saw Sara's handiwork.

"'Felix's Delivery,'" he read proudly. "Thanks, Sara. Too bad we didn't have any gold paint, but you did the lettering way better than I ever would have."

For a split second, Sara knew exactly how the characters in the book *Tom Sawyer* must have felt when Tom conned them into whitewashing the fence!

Ten-year-old Cecily glanced up from where she sat cross-legged, intent on her own work. Felix's younger sister had insisted on being part of the excitement and had spent the better part of the last two days painstakingly embroidering Blackie's name onto a bridle. Her fingers had the pinpricks to show for it. Her last stitch finally finished, she leapt to her feet and proudly showed her work to the horse.

"Here Blackie, I made this 'specially for you," she said.

The big black head swung around and his soft muzzle sniffed at the soft leather with curiosity. It was obvious the horse liked it—so much that he tried to eat it!

"No Blackie!" shrieked Cecily, who successfully pulled it out of the stallion's mouth before any real damage could be done.

Felicity walked swiftly and disapprovingly towards them from the house.

"That horse will eat anything. Just like you, Felix. You make a perfect pair." Felicity stood to one side, obviously disdainful of the whole venture.

"You're just jealous, Felicity, because Blackie and I are going into business." Felix turned his back on her and started to brush Blackie with more vehemence than was probably necessary.

"Felix King. Quit dreaming!" countered his sister loftily. "You have never once in your life finished anything that you started, and I doubt this newest little whim will prove any different."

Sara and Cecily exchanged glances. Much as she liked Felicity, Sara was always amazed at how unbearably holier-than-thou she could be with her brother.

Felix whirled around, his face screwed into an angry scowl. "I'm going to make you eat your words, Felicity. This is going to be the best delivery service in the whole county. Maybe even the whole Island!"

"I'll believe it when I see it," Felicity snapped. "It's much too cold for that baby out here," she scolded. She snatched Daniel from his carriage and carried him towards the house.

"You'll see it, Felicity. You'll see it," a furious Felix called after her, and when she didn't respond, he threw the grooming brush on the ground in frustration.

Unaware of the latest altercation, Alec and Janet strolled contentedly arm in arm across the yard, heading towards the paddock, where they could see Felix and the girls leading Blackie. Hetty King followed along behind her brother and sister-in-law. Janet's initially dubious attitude had turned to smug parental pride, and Hetty had just spent an hour listening to her go on about Felix and his new enterprise. Other than that, she thought, it had been quite a pleasant lunch.

Hetty was, as usual, neat as a pin, in a white starched blouse, crisp plaid wool skirt and jacket, sporting a jaunty straw hat with a cluster of bright red cherries on it. She rolled her eyes when she realized that Janet was once again pursuing her favorite subject, her children, and in particular Felix.

"You were so right, Alec," she gushed, "and I think it's wonderful that you encouraged him. I've never seen Felix so full of enthusiasm...about working, that is."

Alec beamed. "Well, I must admit, it was a pretty clever way to steer him in the right direction."

"You're a simply wonderful father," said Janet, giving his arm a squeeze.

Hetty could stand it no longer. She felt almost compelled to give her unbiased opinion of the whole situation.

"Although I don't quite share your nauseating parental narcissism, I concede that it's about time Felix shouldered some responsibility. And even if it fails, it will be a good experience for him to have to answer to someone outside his family for a change."

Janet gave a little sniff. "Felix won't fail. Anything my boy sets his mind to is bound to succeed." She strode on to join the children at the rail fence that surrounded the paddock, leaving Hetty with indignantly raised eyebrows.

"Felix, dear," Janet called, "I just want you to know that I will be your first customer. I'm expecting a basket of pears to arrive at the general store tomorrow and I'd like Felix's Delivery to pick them up for me."

Felix crossed to the fence with Sara and Cecily, a wide smile lighting up his face.

"For the going rate?"

"For the going rate," replied his mother, looking sideways at Hetty to see her reaction.

Felix followed her gaze. "Have you got anything that needs delivering or picking up, Aunt Hetty?"

"Well...Felix...I..." stammered his aunt, not particularly enjoying being put on the spot and fully aware of Janet's challenging air. "I generally like to look over my purchases myself..."

"Ah c'mon, Aunt Hetty..." wheedled Felix.

"Felix," warned his father, "if your aunt doesn't care to..."

Hetty sighed. She had said she thought it was a good thing for Felix to learn a little responsibility, and by the look on both Janet and Sara's face she knew she would not be let off lightly if she didn't comply.

"Very well then," she conceded. "You could pick up some jars of preserves from Mr. Steele's farm tomorrow morning...on the seventh concession."

Felix grinned. "Consider it done!" He turned and gave his horse a huge hug around his neck. "We're in business, Blackie!"

But Blackie had other things in mind. The artificial cherries on Hetty's hat bounced temptingly within chomping distance, and he proceeded to chomp away. Hetty whirled around, horrified, and, feeling for her hat, realized the cherries were a thing of the past. Cecily and Sara started to giggle, and, as often happens in such cases, it proved to be contagious, so that everyone joined in with gales of laughter. Everyone except Hetty King, that is.

Chapter Six

Felix was not the only one in the King family embarking on new projects. The next morning, in the crisp air of the barn, Alec King was attacking his own goal with patience and perseverance.

"Whoa, there! Easy boy! Calm down now. That's right!" With very slow, deliberate movements, Alec attempted to hook Caesar up to the buggy. Even after many tries, the horse continued to be very nervous and skittish.

A shaft of golden light fell across the barn floor as the door opened and Janet appeared, her egg basket over one arm. She stopped and watched the horse and Alec's attempts to calm it.

"What kind of horse is this, Alec? He looks as if he's never been hitched to a buggy in his life," she observed, plainly critical. She had grown to embrace the idea of Felix's business, but she had still not reconciled herself to what she considered the unnecessary purchase of another horse.

"Well, perhaps not recently," replied Alec. He continued to keep Caesar's origins a secret. "But I'm getting him used to it slowly. He'll calm down. Soon."

The palomino suddenly reared and pulled away sharply, catching Alec off guard.

"Good deal," Janet couldn't help but remark in an 'I told you so' manner as she watched the struggle of man against beast. "Well, you get what you pay for," were her parting words as she headed for the chicken coop. "That's what my father always said."

Alec had no time to reply as Digger, the adopted family dog, came running into the barn. With his tail wagging mischievously, the large golden-haired mutt planted his feet firmly on the hay-covered floor in a half crouch and started to bark at the horse. This was the last straw for Caesar. He shied and reared, neighing and trying desperately to escape the shenanigans of the dog.

"Whoa! Easy fella! Digger! Be quiet!" com-
manded Alec, using all his strength to hold the
horse and keep it from bolting. The fun over,
Digger bounded off in the direction of the chicken
coop to see what other mischief he could get into.

"All right, all right, whoa Caesar. That's
enough for one day. C'mon boy!" Alec finally qui-
eted the horse and led him away.

As he passed a closed stall, the low voice of his
son caught his ear.

"I'll take care of you, Blackie. You'll never have
to leave King Farm."

Alec stopped and listened, unnoticed, watching through a crack in the wood of the stall. Felix
was brushing Blackie to as much of a sheen as is
possible with an old workhorse. He spoke to the
animal in a low, soothing voice.

"No more out to pasture for you. You still got a
lot of good years left. Yes sir! Now stand still,
there's a good boy. I'll bet you haven't had a
grooming like this for a long time. But you have to
look good. We have some deliveries to make this
morning. Here, I've got a reward for you."

Alec shook his head slowly and smiled as Felix
took an apple out of his pocket and sank his teeth
into one side of it. Blackie took a big bite out of the
other side of the apple, taking it right from the

boy's mouth. Felix giggled as the horse's muzzle tickled him.

Alec felt a tightening in his throat and quickly backed around the corner of the stall out of sight as Felix led Blackie out of the barn. The father watched from the shadows as his son hooked the horse up to the newly restored cart, the red lettering of the words "Felix's Delivery" shining in the early morning sunlight. They were in business.

Chapter Seven

Felix struggled gamely under the weight of his mother's bushel basket of pears as he carried them out of the general store.

"What an adorable cart!" Mrs. Lawson declared as she followed him onto the porch, her face lighting up with pleasure. Her expression changed, however, the minute she spied Blackie going straight towards a barrel of apples that was unfortunately within reach. She gently pushed the animal away, but Blackie was determined. He stretched his neck even farther and came within chomping range. Mrs. Lawson pushed Blackie's great head away again, this time not so gently, and with one booted foot moved the temptation from the horse's reach.

"I think we'll have lots of odd delivery jobs for you to do, Felix," Mrs. Lawson said cheerily, one hand on Blackie's harness, still keeping a close eye on the situation. Felix unhooked the back flap of the cart and struggled to slide the large load of pears in without tipping the whole bushel over.

"It makes good business sense for us to offer such a service. We'd gladly pay for it!" Mrs. Lawson continued, as Blackie suddenly shook her hand away and butted her with his head in an attempt to reach the forbidden fruit.

"You know," she remarked to Felix with a knowing look at the apples and the horse, "I think we've paid for part of your service already!"

Felix smiled ruefully and hoisted himself into the driver's seat, pulling Blackie's head back with the reins. Once again, Mrs. Lawson helped the horse along with one hand and tried to move the barrel out of the way with the other.

"No more now! That's enough!" she scolded the unruly animal, managing to keep a brave smile on her face.

Felix waved as horse and buggy moved away into the street.

"There you go," said Mrs. Lawson, with more than a little relief. "Say hello to your mother for me, all right?"

Felix bumped along the seventh concession, happy and carefree. The sun was out, the sky was blue, and the countryside was at its peak of autumn beauty. As far as he could see, this working business was just fine. Felix was oblivious to the fact that behind him, at each major pothole, pears bounced like balls out of the basket and rolled around on the rough bottom of the cart.

An unruly clan of geese scrambled hither and thither in farmer Steele's yard as Felix staggered to his cart with a box filled with jars of preserves of every conceivable variety. How could his Aunt Hetty possibly consume all this jam, he couldn't help but wonder, and stay so everlastingly skinny?

"I hope ya closed the gate behind ya," Mr. Steele growled, and he puffed so hard on his pipe that Felix was immediately enveloped in a cloud of acrid smoke.

"Yes sir, I did," Felix replied, trying not to cough. He thankfully lowered his burden into the bottom of the cart, next to the pears.

Farmer Steele was a sallow, wheezing man who didn't seem to find much in the day to give him pleasure, except reminding people of things they might do wrong.

"Be careful with them jars!" grunted the man, his face scrunched up into a permanent frown. "Your Aunt Hetty always sends her empties back to be refilled. They ain't gonna be much good to me broken!"

Felix rolled his eyes and was about to make a hasty exit when from out of nowhere came a whirling mass of black-and-white fur, barking and snapping at his heels.

The dog took Felix totally by surprise, and he jumped back and tried to defend himself. Farmer Steele puffed on his pipe and remained unconcerned.

"Good boy, good boy," he rasped as the mutt danced and jumped around.

Felix realized with great relief that the dog was not exactly vicious, just playful, but his rambunctiousness made Blackie very nervous, and the horse shied and shifted position, jerking the cart suddenly backwards. The back flap fell down, and since the cart was parked on a slight incline, the pears that had come loose from the bushel basket on the trip from the general store poured out onto the ground and continued to roll on down the hill.

"Oh no!" Felix groaned. He had no choice but to chase after them, with the dog snapping at both his heels and the pears. A momentary panic flooded over him. What would his mother say? He couldn't fail to deliver the goods on his very first day in business! He gathered up an armful of fruit and returned it to the cart. They didn't look too banged-up, he thought, examining them briefly. Besides, his mother only used them for preserves. What were a few bumps and bruises? They got mushed up in the end anyway.

Needless to say, Felix was very glad to see the end of farmer Steele when he finally pulled out of the man's driveway and headed back down the seventh concession towards Avonlea.

The bumpy road, however, once again took its toll, and unbeknownst to Felix, every time he hit a rut the preserve jars bounced a good three inches off the floor of the cart.

"Well, that wasn't so bad, for the first day, Blackie," he commented in a self-satisfied way, unaware of the precarious state of affairs behind him. "I hope everyone doesn't own a vicious dog, though."

Hetty King looked at the watch pinned precisely over her heart and closed the lace curtains of her parlor with an annoyed flick of her wrist. Where was that boy? Why had she let Janet put her in the questionable position of relying on

Felix? She tsked loudly to no one in particular and was about to turn away from the window when the bright-blue cart came into sight around the bend in the road. She smiled in spite of herself. There! What had she been worried about? No nephew of hers could possibly fail to rise to the occasion. Even Felix! She left the parlor and went out the front door to meet the dear boy.

Felix jumped down from the cart and waved gaily at his aunt.

"Well, Felix, how's business?" Hetty called to him as he walked around to fetch her box of preserves from the back of the cart.

"Can't complain," he replied, in the same offhand manner he had heard Hank Webster use. As he followed his aunt into the house, his knees wobbled under the weight of the box.

"Hard work, hmmm? I hope it teaches you that nothing comes easy in this world," Hetty said as she led the way to the kitchen. "Remember, you only reap what you sow."

Hetty King never lost an opportunity to bestow what she considered to be small jewels of enlightenment upon children, whether they were in or out of her classroom.

Felix plunked the box down noisily on the long, polished wooden table.

"You know what, Aunt Hetty, I couldn't agree with you more," he stated emphatically, to the delight of his aunt, who suddenly felt that all the advice she was certain had fallen on deaf ears and been wasted on Felix had finally come to fruition.

"And you know how you're always teaching us to do things all the way and not by halves?" he continued. "Well, there's going to be nothing halfway about this business."

Hetty smiled, as proud as proud could be of her brother's son. There was, after all, some King blood running in the boy's veins, not, as she had sometimes feared, only the Wards'.

"That's good to hear," she said heartily, and she took her change purse from a crockery jar on the window ledge. "There you are, my boy. Cash on the barrel, as they say!"

"Thank you, ma'am," Felix replied with mock seriousness and tipped his hat.

"Aunt Hetty will do nicely, thank you, Felix!" his aunt said good-naturedly as she lifted one of the jars out of the crate. "And don't think I intend to reimburse you for every favor you do for me in the future..." Only then did she feel something wet and sticky running off her hands, onto her skirt and down to her boots.

"Gracious Providence, Felix King! What in heaven's name has happened to my preserves?" she shrieked as the bright-red raspberry jam ran out of the cracked jar onto her previously spotless floor.

She handed the jar immediately to Felix, not knowing where to wipe her hands, and succeeded only in spreading the sticky syrup further. Felix dropped the container onto the table and gingerly moved some of the remaining jars around in the crate. All but a few were completely cracked and broken. He shook his head in innocent bewilderment.

"I wouldn't buy preserves from that Mr. Steele any more if I were you, Aunt Hetty. I knew I couldn't trust the man the minute I laid eyes on him. Besides, anyone with a vicious dog has something to hide."

Hetty hardly heard a word her nephew said, such an absolute state was she in. Each time she wiped jam from one spot it ended up in another.

"Well," she huffed, "it's never happened before!"

In a tizzy she crossed to the sink and began to furiously pump water. Then, through the window, she spotted Blackie happily eating the few remaining blossoms off the pink hydrangea bushes lining her picket fence.

"Stop that horse, Felix!" she shouted. Hetty rushed for the door, with Felix close behind her.

"Blackie! No!" yelled Felix.

"My flowers!" moaned Hetty.

"He's hungry," said Felix, lamely. "I promised him something to eat when we got home."

Hetty fixed him with a piercing gaze. "How does Blackie feel about preserves?"

"Ten, fifteen, twenty-five, fifty, seventy-five, eighty-five, ninety, one dollar!"

Hunched over the kitchen table, Felix carefully counted his money under the watchful eye of an admiring Sara and Cecily.

"A whole dollar?" Cecily breathed.

"I might even have enough to buy Blackie some oats...for a treat!" Felix beamed. He also couldn't help thinking about those skates he wanted in the general store.

Sara picked up a piece of crumpled paper by his elbow. "Is this your list for tomorrow?"

"Yup. I'm going to be busy!" he crowed, scraping the coins into his hand and stacking them in little piles on the table.

"You should advertise, Felix," advised Sara. "My father always said that advertising was crucial to the growth of any business."

The back door slammed and in walked Alec, his face red from the wind that suddenly chilled the cozy room. He glanced at Felix and frowned slightly.

"When are you going to feed the chickens, Felix?"

"I'll do it!" replied Felix, without looking up. "Right after I finish counting this money again."

"Make sure you do," said his father, taking off his coat and hat. "You know our bargain."

"I know, I know!" said Felix, impatiently, under his breath.

At the counter, a frowning Janet sorted through her pears. Some of them looked as if they had been actually nibbled!

"Felicity, have a look at these," she called to her daughter, who was busy kneading bread dough. Felicity wiped her hands on her apron, took a pear out of the basket and eyed it critically.

"I'll have to cut away half of them," complained her mother. "I must have a word with Mrs. Lawson. They're just not up to her usual standards."

Felicity screwed up her pretty little nose in distaste. "They look like they've already been chewed. And look at all the bruises." Felicity turned and looked straight at Felix, her eyes narrowing. "Whatever could have happened to them?" she asked knowingly.

Felix met his sister's accusing gaze without

flinching and, painting an innocent look on his face, said nothing.

Chapter Eight

The cold wind that signaled the approach of winter blew through the streets of Avonlea and ruffled the edges of the new flyer tacked to the big maple tree in front of Mrs. Biggins's boarding house. Most of the leaves were down—only a few stubborn, crimson-red ones clung to the tree's branches—and Sara, Felix and Cecily stood on a patchwork carpet of gold, yellow and amber admiring their work.

"Felix's Delivery Service," read the ad. "Felix King Proprietor."

"That's good, Sara!" said Felix, nodding his head with authority. They had hung signs all the way from the King farm to the village, and they still had a lot to do before the morning school bell rang. "Let's put them up all over town!"

Cecily and Sara ran off in opposite directions, armed with hammer and nails and a stack of neatly printed posters. It had taken Sara almost all night to finish them, much to her Aunt Hetty's disgust. Sara smiled to herself when she thought of her aunt's shocked face, under the brim of her nightcap, when she had discovered her lamp still burning at three o'clock in the morning!

Felix headed across the street and proceeded to tack a sign to a post in front of the blacksmith's shop. Hank Webster and Abner Jeffries and a few other men hung around a fire that burned outside the smithy, warming their hands and enjoying a morning mug of hot, steaming coffee. Hank watched Felix with some amusement and called out to him.

"Hey Felix! Felix King! C'mon over here, boy!"

Felix walked slowly over to the man, who heartily shook his hand.

"Just want to welcome you to the business community of Avonlea, son," Hank said jovially, half tongue-in-cheek. "Don't we, boys?"

Abner slapped Felix on the back. "Hear, hear!" he boomed, smiling over his shoulder at the other men.

"So you've got yourself a little delivery business, eh?" said one, as he elbowed the fellow next to him.

"Yes, I uh…" mumbled Felix, tongue-tied in front of the grown-ups.

Abner interrupted him, winking at Hank. "Better watch yourself, Hank. He might give you a run for your money."

The other men roared with laughter and rocked back and forth on their heels as Felix watched them, not quite knowing how to take all this mirth.

"Well, I enjoy a little competition," replied Hank, his eyes twinkling. "May the best man win, right Felix?"

"Right, Mr. Webster."

Hank slapped him on the back. "Call me Hank, boy. You're one of us now!"

"Right, Mr. Webster...I mean...Hank..."

Once again, the men laughed as they grouped themselves around the fire and continued their previous conversation, seemingly including Felix in their circle. The boy couldn't help but puff up a little with pride. He enjoyed listening to the men talking shop and copied their mannerisms, his fingers stuck in the pockets of his pants, swaggering a bit.

"So what do you think of the new tax there's talk of?" asked one, tapping his pipe out into the fire.

"They'll tax the life right out of the economy if they don't watch it!" Abner observed wisely, scratching his head.

"Did you see how high the price of wheat has gone?" observed another.

"As long as it still needs deliverin' I ain't complainin'," guffawed Hank, turning to the boy standing next to him. "Right, Felix?"

"Right, Mr. Webster!...Hank," replied Felix, staunchly.

"I'm pullin' in my horns. Planted half the potatoes that I did last year," stated one of the men flatly, and he spat on the ground to emphasize his point.

"That's a fool thing to do," said Abner, unimpressed.

Hank Webster agreed. "Business has to expand to remain healthy in these times. I've hired another driver," he boasted.

Felix pulled himself to his full height. "The only way to expand any business is to advertise," he said, determined to get his two cents in. "And that's what I'm doing."

The men stared as Felix reached into his pocket. "My card," he said, handing one to each of them. "Tack it up where you can see it. Morning, gentlemen."

Felix swaggered away, leaving the men doubled over in silent laughter.

"My card...?" wheezed Abner, holding it up and staring at it short-sightedly.

"Do you believe it?" hooted the man next to him.

They all laughed and slapped each other on the back.

Only Hank Webster watched as Felix disappeared down the street. "Well, good for him," he said gruffly, and he looked at the card in his hand, smiling, his gold tooth glinting in the morning sun.

Chapter Nine

Janet King climbed up the back stairs, a load of folded laundry in her hands. The baby was having an afternoon nap and she had finally found the time to do the ironing. She breathed in deeply, enjoying the scent of the freshly laundered shirts and bedclothes, still warm in her arms from the iron. There was something strangely satisfying about it, even though, of all her household tasks, the never-ending stream of laundry always seemed the most dreadfully daunting.

She tiptoed by the room where the baby lay sleeping and arrived at Felix's closed bedroom door. There was a sign on it, "Felix's Delivery." Janet couldn't help but smile. Felix had certainly taken this job seriously.

"Bless his heart," she said to herself as she opened the door and went in.

A very indignant Felix looked up at his mother as she entered, an annoyed frown on his face. His shirtsleeves were held up by two black bands above his elbows, and he wore a little visor, much like the one he had seen the foreman at the track in Summerside wear. He had turned one of the deepest drawers of his dresser upside down, and its flat surface provided a makeshift desk, which he now sat behind, facing Sara and Cecily. Digger lay at his feet and looked up lazily as Janet bustled around the room, putting her son's laundry away.

"Mother!" said Felix, obviously very put out. "We are having an important business meeting!"

Janet raised her eyebrows and put a stack of clean shirts on her son's bed.

"Oh..." she said in mock seriousness. "I'm very sorry dear, but..."

Felix did not appreciate his mother's amused and condescending smile. He found her attitude incredibly irritating, especially in front of Sara and Cecily. Didn't she realize he wasn't a baby any more? It was about time she started taking this business of his seriously.

"Would you kindly knock before entering in the future?"

Felix's tone of voice cut through any gentle tolerance Janet may have had. "Felix King, I'm your mother! You watch the way you speak to me. I shouldn't have to knock just to put laundry in your bedroom..."

"This is an office by day," Felix reminded her severely.

Janet was more than a little taken aback. If Sara and Cecily had not been staring at her with their big blue eyes, she might have been tempted to tell Felix just what she thought of his attitude. As it was, she decided to let it go for the moment. Giving him one last look of motherly warning, she put the rest of his laundry on the bed and left the room in silence. She passed Felicity in the hall and continued into her daughter's room with her load, which, for some reason, seemed a lot heavier.

His mother out of the way, Felix turned back to the meeting at hand.

"As I was saying," he began, with the self-important air of someone who has been rudely interrupted, "based on the success of my first week in business, I have decided to take on some partners."

Sara and Cecily exchanged expectant glances. In a voice that eerily echoed Hank Webster's, Felix continued. "It is my belief that business always has to expand in order to be healthy in these economic times."

Cecily looked at him blankly. "What do you mean, Felix?"

"The only thing that is expanding around here is Felix's head," Felicity observed dryly from where she stood at the door.

Felix whirled around in a fury. He hadn't heard his sister come in.

"Don't you know how to knock?" Felix yelled.

Felicity ignored him and turned her attentions to her little sister. "Don't get fooled into working for him, Cecily," she advised coolly, with an air of expertise that only an older sister can muster.

Felix was seething. "You're just in a knot, Felicity, because you know I wouldn't give you the chance to be part of my business even if you paid me!"

"I wouldn't give you two cents for your so-called business, Felix," said Felicity haughtily.

"Just get out!" yelled Felix, jumping up and banging his shins painfully on his desk.

"Gladly," said Felicity as she sailed from the room.

Felix took dead aim and threw a shoe at her, and both Sara and Cecily jumped when it hit the door with a loud thump just as it closed behind her.

Unfazed, Felix sat down behind his desk and continued. "Now. You were asking me what I meant about expanding my business. Well, it's really very simple, Cecily. If I have more people working for me, I can make more deliveries. If I make more deliveries, I make more money."

"Oh," was all Cecily said, and she turned to look at Sara.

"So, would you care to join in my business endeavor?" Felix looked at the two girls expectantly, one eyebrow raised in what he hoped would come across as a stern and businesslike manner.

Sara leaned forward, both elbows on top of the desk. "What would our return be?"

"A small share of the profit." replied Felix crisply. He had expected Sara to ask such a question and he was ready.

"An equal share of the profit," said Sara, her eyes glittering coldly. "Split three ways."

Felix jumped up from the desk. "What? I'm the one who built the business up. You can't have an equal share!"

"It will give us more incentive, Felix," Sara countered firmly, not giving way. "That's what my father always said."

Felix scowled and considered the point. He knew he needed the two girls to accomplish his goal.

"Well…" he began slowly. "We'll do it on a trial basis. That's what my father always says. Agreed?"

Sara and Cecily exchanged looks and nodded.

"Agreed!" said Cecily.

"Agreed," said Sara, and they all shook hands. "Partners."

Digger barked his approval.

Chapter Ten

The very next day, the words "and Company" were carefully added to the "'Felix's Delivery'" sign on the cart.

"'And Company'," said Sara, putting the paintbrush and paint away. "That's better!"

Since Digger had been present at the partnership meeting, he too was immediately pressed into service. Cecily's little red wagon was rigged up with a harness and festooned with the sign "Felix and Company Delivery."

"Digger! Hold still!" said Felix crossly as he attempted to hook the huge dog up to the smaller wagon. The dog was not being cooperative. He kept turning in circles as Felix tried again and again to put the harness on him.

"There's a good boy!" said Cecily, patting Digger's golden head, trying to get him to stand still. "Oh, don't you look handsome!"

The task was finally accomplished and the three stood back to survey their fleet.

"We're going to be rich!" Felix chortled to himself.

Daniel sat in his carriage, a biscuit in each hand, fascinated by the comings and goings of the older children. He dropped one of his biscuits on his blanket and fumbled to pick it up. Instantly, a large black muzzle was in the baby's lap, and to Daniel's delight, Blackie finished the biscuit off with one gulp.

"Blackie! No!" yelled Felix. He shook his head ruefully. The damage was already done.

The children turned to see a relatively triumphant Alec leading Caesar in from the field, hooked up to the buggy.

"There, there fella," he crooned. "That's fine now! Cecily, keep Digger away."

Felix smiled. "You finally got him hitched up!" he observed, not trying terribly hard to keep the sarcasm out of his voice.

"Yes, I did," replied his father.

"He'll never be a match for Blackie!" Sooner or later, thought Felix, his father would have to admit which horse was superior.

Alec smirked at his son and, letting go of Caesar's bridle, he ambled over to see what the children were up to.

Janet chose that moment to come from the house and ring the lunch bell.

"Dinner's ready!" she called.

The minute Caesar heard the bell, he immediately took off at a gallop, buggy and all. Alec whirled around to see the horse disappearing down the driveway.

"Felix, go after him!" he shouted.

Felix was busy holding onto Blackie's reins. "Sara, go after him!" he yelled.

"Me?" squeaked Sara. How could she ever stop a runaway horse and buggy?

An obedient Cecily gamely ran down the lane after Caesar. Digger was at her heels, harness flying, barking furiously, wagon in tow. Sara sighed and followed.

"Alec King!" Janet shouted as her husband ran by her in hot pursuit. "That horse is so jumpy! I'll never trust myself with him!"

"He's still a bit skittish, that's all!" called Alec over his shoulder.

"Skittish! He took off like a racehorse!" replied his wife.

"Well no wonder! With you ringing that bell..."

Alec's words disappeared into the wind as he ran down the driveway.

"What has a bell got to do with it?" called an exasperated Janet. Alec's reply couldn't be heard, and she turned to Felix, who stood holding Blackie's reins. He wore a strange expression, one that told his mother he knew more than he was saying.

"What has a bell got to do with it?" she repeated.

"Nothing...nothing..." replied Felix, his face blank with innocence.

"Caesar! Come back!" Alec's voice floated back to them over the fields.

Later that afternoon, in front of the general store, Felix leaned against the seat of his cart, feet up, reading a newspaper. Blackie almost appeared to be dozing. There was nothing to hold his interest. The bushels of apples had wisely been taken inside.

Felix stretched a bit to see what Sara was up to. He enjoyed being a proprietor of a business. So far, it seemed to mean that he could sit back and relax a bit and let his partners do the work. He returned to his newspaper.

Sara had indeed been hard at work. She had set up a little table in a corner of the general store and on it was a sign, "Felix and Company Delivery Service." She had settled herself to take orders, a price list tacked to the wall behind her, when a beaming Mrs. Lawson led a lady over to her.

"Good morning, Sara. This is Mrs. Wilkes. Right on time!" She smiled at the portly woman next to her. "She's your first customer, Sara. Mrs. Wilkes needs a parcel delivered this afternoon." She handed Sara a package wrapped in brown paper and tied with string.

Sara beamed at the woman. "That's what we're here for, Mrs. Wilkes!"

Mrs. Lawson and Mrs. Wilkes shared an amused smile.

"Isn't it wonderful to see children being so industrious?" said Mrs. Lawson.

The woman nodded, and Sara took up pen and paper in a businesslike manner.

"Thank you for letting us set up here, Mrs. Lawson. I owe you a great debt of gratitude. Now, Mrs. Wilkes, I'll just need some information."

Back at the King farm, having finally found and corralled Caesar, a very tired Alec King strolled into the barn, only to be attacked by a herd of starving and squawking chickens. Nonplussed, he walked over to the feed trays, picked one up and discovered it was completely empty.

"What is going on?" he asked out loud. In his mind, his question was immediately answered. "Felix!" With a sigh of annoyance, he proceeded to feed the hungry chickens as they clustered around him, clucking their own disapproval at the state of things.

Oblivious to his forgotten chores, Felix and Blackie traveled down a winding road that looked over the unending blue of the ocean.

The weather had turned quite warm. It was one of those treasured and rare days between autumn and winter, when summer makes its presence felt, not only reminding us of what we are missing, but also giving us a taste of what we can look forward to.

Farther down the road, trying in vain to keep up, trudged Cecily, straining to control Digger as he pulled the little wagon, heaped with boxes, in Felix's wake.

Chapter Eleven

As so often happens when a goal is set, the means to the end sometimes takes precedence over the end itself. In Felix's case, the goal of successfully taking over the care of his beloved Blackie slowly and insidiously began to be replaced by the means to that end—making money.

Over the week that followed his newly formed partnership with Sara and Cecily, Felix was amazed by the way the returns of their labor multiplied. He became obsessed and more than a little pompous with his success. The other members of the family were beginning to lose patience with him, to say the least.

❧❧❧

"'Felix's Delivery,'" Felix read proudly. "Thanks, Sara. Too bad we didn't have any gold paint, but you did the lettering better than I would have."

❧❧❧

The artificial cherries on Hetty's hat bounced
temptingly within chomping distance.

❧❧❧

Felix struggled to his feet. A wave of panic rose
in his throat. Blackie! He staggered over
to the animal.

⌘⌘⌘

Felix clung tightly to his father, his eyes on the bridle
hanging in the stall.

"One dollar, one dollar and five cents, one dollar and ten cents, one dollar and thirty-five cents…" Felix counted his earnings at the kitchen table, with Cecily and Sara hanging over his shoulder. It had become a nightly ritual.

"Where's our share?" asked Sara.

"Part of that's mine…and Sara's," said Cecily, reaching for some of the coins.

Felix hit her hand away. "Shh! Both of you! I'll lose count!" he hissed at them. "One dollar and forty cents…"

"Well, it is ours. We earned it!" repeated Cecily vehemently, and before her brother could stop her, she started to collect what she reasoned was their share.

"Put it back, Cecily!" yelled Felix. "I can't give you anything until I figure out what it costs to keep Blackie in feed." He stopped and looked at the piles of money in front of him. "Oh great. Now I've lost count."

Alec came in from outside and threw off his coat and hat. As he headed for the sink to wash up, he glanced at the three children around the table, taking in the sullen expressions on their faces. Janet rolled her eyes at him, indicating that her level of tolerance had just about been reached.

"That's not fair," whined Cecily. "I worked harder than you today!"

"One dollar, one dollar and five cents, one dollar and thirty-five cents, one dollar and forty cents…" Felix began the process again, trying to ignore Cecily and Sara.

"Felix! Come on!" yelled Sara, and with Cecily's help she started to take the money away from Felix.

"Children! Stop it right now," said Janet sharply. Her hands were full of silverware and plates to set the dinner table and there was no place to put them.

"Well, it isn't fair!" shouted Cecily, stamping her foot.

"I told you so, Cecily," said Felicity coolly from her place at the stove.

"Felix, could you possibly do that somewhere else? I'd like to set the table for dinner," said a very impatient Janet .

"Shh!" said Felix with annoyance. "I've already lost count once…one dollar and forty-five cents…"

Alec swung around from the sink. Enough was enough. "Felix! Do what your mother tells you!" he said sharply.

"For someone who can add up money so quickly," said Felicity in a voice that carried across the room, "I can't think why you would have failed that mathematics test we had at school today."

The sentence hung in the air. Alec and Janet exchanged looks over the children's heads. Felicity smiled like a cat with a canary as Felix glared at her across the room.

"Felix King!" said his mother. "Now, you promised that you wouldn't sacrifice your school-work for the sake of this business!"

"Or your chores," Alec reminded his son severely. "I had to feed the chickens because some-one forgot to do it…again."

"All right! All right!" grumbled Felix, clearing up his money. "When I'm a millionaire it will hardly matter that I made a few mistakes on a mathematics test or forgot to feed the chickens one day!"

Furious at all of them, he stomped out of the room, leaving Janet and Alec staring after him and then at each other, wondering what had become of their son.

Chapter Twelve

The kitchen in Rose Cottage was filled with the heavenly aroma of home baking. Fresh bread and rolls cooled on the counter, and a beautifully iced chocolate cake stood on a crystal platter in the middle of the table. Hetty walked briskly into the room, opened the oven and checked on an elderberry pie to see if it was ready yet. Deciding that it wasn't quite the golden brown it should be, she put it back in the oven and closed the door.

As she turned, she was just about knocked off her feet by Sara, who rushed in, her nose buried in a list, not looking where she was going. She grabbed her hat from where she had thrown it the night before and flew out of the kitchen to the hall, talking to herself all the way.

"Aunt Abigail's china on the three o'clock train. Mrs. Potts…Mr. Gillis at the lumber mill…"

Hetty stood quite still for a moment, not sure whether it had been Sara who passed her or a small tornado.

"Sara," she called, giving chase, "I wanted to have a few words with you."

She caught up with her niece just as she was taking the stairs up to the second floor two at a time.

"Sara, come back here!" ordered Hetty, in her best schoolmistress voice.

"I'm sorry, Aunt Hetty," Sara's voice floated down. "I have to copy these lists out for Cecily and Felix."

"I need your help polishing the silver. I'm having a few of the ladies over and…"

Sara rushed down the stairs again and past her aunt.

"Really, this constant confusion!" muttered Hetty. "Will you please stay in one spot so I can talk to you!"

There was a sharp knock on the door, and Sara ran to it, dragging her coat on at the same time.

"Wait till they see all these new orders," she said, without looking once in Hetty's direction.

"Sara!" Hetty repeated with extreme annoyance, but her niece had already disappeared out the door.

Hetty straightened her shoulders, like a general going to war, and followed her. But just as she opened the door, the unmistakable scent of burning pastry met her nostrils.

"My pie!" she hissed under her breath, and she ran to the kitchen.

Outside, surrounded by the drooping remains of what had been a glorious summer display of flowers, Sara was in the process of organizing Felix and Cecily with a list of delivery jobs.

"So Felix," she said, with an air of authority, "do the order at the lumber mill first and then Mrs. Potts's order from the general store. She's too sick to pick it up, apparently. Then, to the train station

for Aunt Abigail. And Cecily, you have three gro-
cery pick ups at the general store, including Aunt
Hetty's.

"I can't do all that with this little cart!" Cecily
cried. "It's not fair. Felix gets the big cart all the
time."

For once, Felix didn't jump angrily to his own
defense. He was too busy scanning the list Sara
had handed him.

"There's way too many orders here!" he complained. "You'll have to do some of them, Sara."

"I can't!" his cousin replied emphatically. "I'm
too busy. Do you have any idea how hard it is sitting at a desk taking orders all day long? You're
lucky. At least you get to be outside!"

Having rescued what was left of her pie, Hetty
finally made it outside and interrupted what
would most certainly have escalated into a full-
fledged fight.

"Cecily," she said sternly, "if I have to put up
with you three swarming around like bees, the least
I can expect is for *my* groceries to be delivered *first*!
Now, make sure you're back with them by four
o'clock. The ladies from the Improvement Society
are coming for dinner and I have a stew to make."

Hetty stopped, horrified, as she watched
Blackie take an apple straight from Felix's mouth.

"Felix King, have you any idea how many germs lie festering in a horse's mouth? The next thing you know, you'll be getting lockjaw!"

"I hope he does!" said Cecily, sticking her tongue out at him.

Felix glared at his sister and, hopping into his cart, set off with Blackie. Sara ran along beside him, leaping in at the last minute.

"Sara!" Hetty called after her niece. "I need your help to set the table!"

"I can't, Aunt Hetty," Sara yelled back. "I have to go to the store!"

Cecily watched the cart go down the road, her bottom lip set in a permanent pout. Then she shrugged and set off with Digger and the wagon.

Hetty stood at her fence, shaking her head. She glanced down at the sorry state of her garden and began vigorously plucking the dead blooms from her flowers. That horse must have been at them again, she thought to herself. What would the ladies of the Improvement Society ever think?

Archie Gillis spotted the blue cart approaching the lumber mill and went out onto the platform to meet his delivery. He couldn't help but be a bit envious of Alec King. He must be one proud father. Why couldn't his own boy show some of Felix

King's gumption? Rupert was as lazy as a bedbug and twice as stupid, Archie thought ruefully to himself. The only thing he showed any interest in at all was fighting and hockey. Mostly fighting.

Blackie snorted as Felix pulled on the reins, and taking a package out of the cart, he handed it to the owner of the lumber mill.

"Here you are, Mr, Gillis, sir."

"Good man. I've been waiting a long time for this." Archie reached his hand deep into his pocket and withdrew some change.

"Thank you," Felix said as he cheerfully pocketed the coins. "C'mon Blackie!" Felix clucked his tongue and horse and buggy headed off towards the town of Avonlea and the indisposed Mrs. Potts.

Archie ripped open his package, thinking to himself the new saw blades would surely come in handy.

"What the…?" the poor man exclaimed.

A group of workers gathered around him and broke out into great guffaws as Archie Gillis held up what appeared to be a lady's corset, in an extremely generous size!

"You been waiting a long time for that, have ya, Archie?" said one of his men, slapping his knee with glee.

"It's your size all right!" said another, and the group broke up with howls of laughter.

The decidedly rotund Archie Gillis was as red as a beet as he stuffed the offending garment back into the package and stormed back into his mill.

It was almost four o'clock by the time an exhausted Cecily finally came back along the road beside the King pond, pulling Digger by the collar. The little wagon filled with Aunt Hetty's groceries bumped along behind them.

"Hurry Digger! Aunt Hetty'll be mad if we're late."

Cecily sighed. She was tired, her feet hurt, she was angry at Felix, and she was even angry at Sara, whom she usually adored. But Sara, she thought to herself severely, was not working as hard as the other two partners. She had the easy job of sitting behind a desk in the general store.

Suddenly, right in front of her, a duck flew out of the bushes near the pond and startled Cecily out of her reverie. Digger was taken by surprise, too. No sooner had he spotted the bird than he was instantly on the run, pulling the bouncing cart behind him, down the grassy bank to the pond.

"Digger! No!" screamed Cecily, running after him. "Digger! Come back!"

It was too late. The duck hit the water at the same time the dog did. Digger's nose twitched with the instincts of the hunter and he splashed headlong through the pond, cart and all. He galloped towards the duck who, of course, hearing the commotion, rose quacking into the air just as the golden dog reached it.

Cecily stared in dismay at the wreckage. The little wagon had tipped over. Her Aunt Hetty's groceries floated in the pond...and then, item by item, they sank to the bottom.

As Felix walked away from her house whistling, Mrs. Potts rose from her sick bed to unwrap her newly delivered package. The poor woman was convalescing from a bout of influenza, and she was extremely grateful to Felix's service for saving her a trip to the general store. She dearly needed the undergarment she had ordered some weeks ago from the catalogue.

For a moment she wondered how the parcel could possibly be so heavy, but she was soon to realize the reason why. She stared open-mouthed at the saw blades that fell from the wrapping.

Oblivious, Felix climbed up onto his buggy and drove away.

Sara sat at her desk facing an irate Archie Gillis, who waved a crunched-up parcel in front of her nose. To her extreme embarrassment, a few curious people gathered around whispering and smirking behind their hands.

"Now see here, miss! Who's been tinkerin' around with my order? You got it all mixed up somehow and I aim to get to the bottom of it!"

Sara swallowed hard and blushed to the tips of her ears. "What exactly got mixed up?"

"Well...I didn't get what I was supposed to get!" Mr. Gillis said abruptly, obviously not wanting to go into very much detail.

"What did you get?" insisted Sara. "I need to see it, because then I'll know where your things went, by mistake."

It was Archie Gillis's turn to blush as he unwillingly opened his package and held up the corset. Sudden laughter erupted, and the man whirled around to face the crowd of curious onlookers who were now overcome with mirth.

The poor man was mortified. The package, however, was suddenly and rudely ripped out of his hands by an even more humiliated and upset Mrs. Potts, who had entered the store unnoticed.

"Here are your blasted saw blades!" she puffed, thrusting them at Archie. Then she hurriedly stuffed the corset into her basket and glared at Sara. The poor woman was looking a little the worse for wear from her flu, hair flying out from her head at odd angles, her face splotchy with anger.

"I will not forget this to the end of my days, Sara Stanley!"

Mrs. Potts stormed out of the store without uttering another word, which was extremely unusual for her.

Sara bit her lip as the laughing crowd dispersed, leaving her on her own at her little desk. Her father had always said there were good days and bad days in any business. This had definitely been one of the bad ones.

Chapter Thirteen

Felix leapt to his feet, almost upsetting his makeshift desk.

"What do you mean we don't have any pickups or deliveries lined up for the next few days? Why?"

He was chairing an emergency meeting of Felix and Company Delivery Service, and a definite impasse had been reached among the partners. Only Digger seemed unconcerned as he lay, drooling and panting, between a very defensive Sara and Cecily.

Sara stood up and faced her scowling cousin. "There aren't any orders, Felix," she said, slowly and clearly, "because all I've listened to all day is complaints. Even in my own household. Aunt Hetty was furious! Her groceries ended up in the pond!"

"In the pond?" Felix immediately turned on Cecily. "How could you do such a stupid thing?"

"It wasn't my fault," she cried. "Digger's not used to being hooked up to a stupid cart!"

"You're supposed to be in charge of the stupid dog!" Felix shouted back at his sister.

"Digger's not stupid!" yelled Cecily, jumping to her feet.

"Well somebody is!" Felix shot back, looking pointedly at Cecily, who was on the verge of tears.

Sara had had just about enough of Felix's bullying. "You aren't so smart yourself, Felix King! You got all Mrs. Lawson's deliveries mixed up."

Felix's face was turning a shade of vermilion. "If you'd gotten the orders straight in the first place, it wouldn't have happened!" he shouted, throwing down a pencil in disgust. He narrowed his eyes and looked from his sister to his cousin. "I guess this is what I get for letting you two have any part of my business!"

"Oh, is that so!" said Sara, becoming increasingly angry.

"What a mean thing to say, Felix!" sobbed Cecily, wiping her nose with the back of her hand.

"We quit!" announced Sara vehemently. "Right Cecily?"

"Right!" agreed Cecily tearfully. "We quit!" She looked down at the beloved golden head at her feet. "And so does Digger!"

Digger barked his agreement, and the girls flounced out the door, the big dog following them.

Felix's rage boiled over as he watched them go. "Fine!" he yelled after them. "I was better off without you in the first place!"

His bedroom door slammed shut. Felix sat down behind his desk and hit it hard with his fist. He immediately pulled his hand away, soaking wet!

"Yecch! Drool!" he exclaimed, and he wiped the surface with his sleeve. "Stupid dog!"

Felicity King had not been able to ignore the unmistakable sounds of a fight coming from Felix's bedroom, and so she had been standing outside the closed door, eavesdropping, when the two furious girls stormed by her and down the stairs. She smiled to herself, and something inside urged her on. Without any hesitation, she walked into Felix's bedroom.

Felix glared up at her from the place of authority behind his desk. At least, he thought of it as a desk. All his older sister saw was an overturned dresser drawer.

"I told you to knock!" he yelled. "Get out!"

"Having trouble, Mr. Big Businessman? Is that mutiny I smell in the air?" Felicity smiled sweetly at him, making him more furious than ever.

"Felicity, be quiet!" Felix looked around for something to throw.

"You shouldn't blame Sara and Cecily for your lack of business," Felicity continued demurely, in a voice that would melt butter.

"Will you just get out, Felicity?" warned her brother.

"Oh, dear Felix," scolded his sister irritatingly. "I think it's time you listened to your older sibling... before you get really hurt. You thought you were such a big shot. Didn't you realize that your only customers were your relatives and friends? And couldn't you see they were only doing it to humor you?"

"That's not true!" Felix denied it hotly, but a tiny, stubborn seed of doubt had been planted.

"Oh yes it is," continued an unrelenting Felicity. "They were all laughing at you behind your back. Everyone but you knows that! How many times did you think you could deliver damaged goods?

If you were a real delivery company you wouldn't have lasted a day!"

Felix had listened to all he was going to. Without a word, he stomped out of his room in a rage. He would never admit it, even to himself, but he was as close to tears as he had ever been. Over his dead body would he give Felicity the pleasure of seeing that.

Felicity lifted her chin and gave a little sniff. A small voice inside her said reasonably that someone had to tell him, the little know-it-all. He deserved it, she said to herself. But now that she'd done it, she wasn't enjoying the victory quite as much as she'd thought she would.

Chapter Fourteen

It had been a very silent dinner in the King household. Alec and Janet had, as usual, discussed the events of the day and plans for the next, but the three oldest children were noticeably silent, sullen and withdrawn. Only baby Daniel gurgled happily in his high chair, succeeding in wearing more of his dinner than he ate.

The minute the dishes had been collected and washed, Felix had disappeared, and Felicity and

Cecily had gone quietly to their room, not speaking to each other.

Having just finished putting Daniel into his nightgown, Alec was startled by a sharp rapping at the front door. He listened to hear if anyone else in the house would answer it, but the knocking continued, only louder. Alec sighed as he picked up the baby and headed down the stairs to the front hall.

"All right! We're coming!" he called, wondering where in heaven's name everyone else had disappeared to.

Before he could even reach the front door, his sister stuck her head around its corner and walked in.

"Hetty! What brings you here?" Alec was quite surprised. It was dark out. Hetty rarely ventured from Rose Cottage after dusk.

Without a word of greeting, the irate Hetty handed an itemized list to Alec.

"What's this?" he asked, thoroughly puzzled.

"A bill!" she replied tersely, and she proceeded to read it out. " 'One hat. Three dozen eggs....' Four bags of groceries." She looked up at Alec over the rim of her glasses. "They ended up at the bottom of the pond, and I ended up serving leftovers to the ladies of the Improvement Society."

She took her glasses off and replaced them neatly in their case. "I wasn't going to say anything," she began, "but I sat and stewed all evening, listening to Sara's tales of woe, and I'll not let it pass without saying something."

Alec was still completely in the dark. "What are you talking about?" he asked, shifting a squirming Daniel to his other shoulder.

"Your son, Alec King, that's what!" Hetty said with an exasperated sigh. "This delivery business has got out of hand. I don't know what kind of father you are not to have noticed. I am certainly relieved that Sara no longer has anything to do with it."

"What are you talking about, Hetty?" Alec repeated once again, beginning to believe he was as dull-witted as Hetty obviously thought he was.

"I would like to be reimbursed," replied Hetty bluntly, giving up trying to explain things to Alec.

Janet came down the stairs and peered over Alec's shoulder at the list in his hand. She heaved a sigh and looked at her sister-in-law with barely disguised impatience.

"Oh Hetty, you're making such a fuss over nothing. Adults should stay out of children's affairs. It's far better that they straighten out their own problems by themselves."

"They can straighten out their own problems as much as they like," said an exasperated Hetty, "but when it comes to my problems I expect a little adult intervention!"

"Oh for heaven's sake," said Alec as he handed Janet the baby. He took his wallet out of his back pocket and handed some bills and change to his sister.

"Here!" he said, extremely annoyed. "I know it's beyond your experience, but I think you should remember that boys have to do things the hard way before they learn the right way. That's what father always said."

"And like a lot of things father said regarding children, that was a load of hooey!" replied Hetty, counting the money to make sure it was the correct amount. "God rest his soul," she added. Then she handed Alec back a few pennies. "Too much!" she stated flatly, and in a wink she was out the door.

Alec stared at the coins in his hand. "Too much," he muttered. Turning to Janet for moral support, he was surprised to see that she was frowning at him. Had he said something wrong?

The barn was quiet, save for the rustling of the chickens on their roosts and the wind whistling through chinks in the walls. Felix made his way towards the stalls, bathed in a pool of light from the hurricane lamp he carried.

"Blackie!" he called quietly, and a soft whinny of recognition answered his voice. Blackie stirred at the sound of Felix approaching, and when the boy entered the stall the great black horse nuzzled him, his warm breath tickling Felix's neck. He was obviously pleased to see him. Unlike everyone else in his entire household, thought Felix, feeling more than a little sorry for himself.

The boy hugged the horse tightly and produced a carrot from his pocket. Blackie bit off the top of it as Felix held it out to her, and forgetting entirely his Aunt Hetty's warnings of rampaging germs and lockjaw, Felix took the next bite and handed the rest to the horse. He smiled as Blackie chewed contentedly. It was warm and comfortable in the stall. Maybe he would just live out here, thought Felix. Then he wouldn't have to talk to Felicity or his mother and father ever again.

He picked up the grooming brush from a ledge in the stall and began to brush Blackie slowly and thoroughly until the animal turned a glossy black. With each stroke, Felix's hurt feelings began to heal.

"I want a word with you, young man."

Felix was so startled, he almost dropped the brush as he swung around. Alec stood there, and it appeared that he was not entirely happy. Felix looked up at his father and then away, not saying anything.

"This delivery business of yours has got out of hand," began his father after a pause.

Felix felt his face go red, and anger started to boil up inside him once again. "Cecily's a little blabbermouth," was all he said.

"Cecily hasn't said a word," replied his father.

All the frustration that had built up in Felix over the past few days burst out in a torrent. "Nobody thinks I can do anything around here! You're all just waiting for me to mess up!"

"Now look, son," replied Alec firmly, looking Felix straight in the eye, "we had an agreement, and so far you're not living up to your end of it. You're not keeping up with your schoolwork. I've been doing most of your chores. Hetty's just come by with a bill for damaged goods a mile long..."

"I'll pay it," replied Felix sullenly.

Alec heaved a sigh. He had come into the barn to have a quiet and reasonable conversation with his son about the bargain they had made and the responsibility that went with it, but Felix's sudden surliness and obvious belief that paying somebody back was all it took to make everything right caught him by surprise. He was suddenly very disappointed in his son, and his disappointment quickly turned to anger.

"With what?" Alec demanded. "Is that what it's all about now? Money? I thought this was about Blackie."

Felix whirled around defensively. "It is!"

Alec shook his head. "No! You're not doing this for Blackie any more! You're doing it for Felix!" he snapped, his voice rising. "Well, I'll tell you! It's over. Finished. This is it!"

Suddenly, Felix felt cold. "What do you mean?"

"You're out of business," said Alec. "As of now!"

Giving his son one last look, Alec turned and walked out of the barn.

Felix stood stock-still. He felt as if he had been struck a blow. He had never seen his father quite so angry. He was about to call after him, beg him for a second chance, but the disappointment he felt was overcome by anger and resentment.

He moved back into the stall and stroked Blackie's head, fighting back tears. "Let him say what he wants, Blackie, but you and I are a team. We'll show him. We'll show them all."

Janet was knitting by the fire in the cozy King farm kitchen when Alec came back in, slamming the door behind him. Janet watched her husband as he hung up his coat and hat. She could tell, just by the way he held his shoulders, that things had not gone well.

"Did you talk to him?" she asked.

"Yes," replied Alec, tersely.

"Well?"

"Well what?"

"What did you say?" She waited expectantly.

Alec sighed. "Janet, I can't just repeat verbatim what I said."

His wife put her knitting down and sighed. "So you didn't talk! You just got angry."

"No, I didn't just get angry!" huffed Alec, wishing she wasn't so close to the truth.

"You said you wouldn't," said Janet, taking up her knitting once again and attacking it with new vigor. "Really Alec, I know you and your father found it difficult to say two words in a row to each other, but—"

"That has nothing to do with it!" Alec interrupted.

"And..." continued Janet, ignoring his tone of voice, "you've always been wonderful with the children. However, in this case, I'm beginning to agree with Hetty."

Alec made a pretense of shaking his head, trying to clear out his ears. "This can't be," he said, in mock amazement.

Janet put her knitting in its basket and stood up, hands on her hips. "Contrary to your father's belief, Alec, boys don't always have to learn the hard way."

Alec was about to interrupt, but Janet continued. "What they could use most is a little guidance...and not someone simply shouting at them!"

"I didn't just shout at him!" Alec said, his voice a little louder than he had meant it to be.

"Well, you're shouting at me! Good night." Janet grabbed her knitting basket and left the room in a huff. Alec looked at the ceiling and let his breath out in a long, low whistle.

He didn't want to admit it quite yet, but what Janet had said about his father bothered him. She had struck a nerve, and he suddenly found himself unsure.

Chapter Fifteen

"Felix, hurry up!" called Felicity, crossing the yard with Cecily. "You're going to be late for school!"

Felix looked up from feeding the chickens. "I'll catch up with you in a minute," he yelled, and he watched as his sisters waved and continued down the driveway. The minute they disappeared from sight, Felix dumped the entire pail of feed in front of the startled chickens and ran to the barn, where Blackie was already hitched to the cornflower-blue delivery cart.

It was a beautiful, bright, crisp day, and the unsettling arguments of the night before faded away. Felix's mind was filled with the need to show everyone that he could do what he had set out to do, whether he was allowed to or not. After all, who were *they* to tell him what to do? His father and Felicity didn't understand. How could they? he reasoned. Of everyone in the family, they had been the least involved with "Felix's Delivery."

It was easy for Felix to rationalize his decision. He had tasted the one sweet aspect of responsibility—freedom—and he was not about to give it up easily.

Blackie pulled the cart slowly and contentedly along the back roads that led to Avonlea, a whistling Felix holding his reins. They clattered under the covered bridge and into town. When they reached the blacksmith's shop, Felix noticed that Hank Webster and the same group of men were gathered around the fire.

He pulled up and jumped down from the cart, expecting to be included once again in their manly talk. But the men smiled and winked at each other as he approached.

"So I hear Archie Gillis at the mill is the proud owner of some pretty fancy undergarments!" said Hank. "Is that right, Felix? I would have given anything to be there!"

The other men laughed heartily, and Felix felt his face starting to flush.

Abner dug his elbow into Hank's ribs. "And I hear that advertisin' isn't always the ticket to expandin' your business!"

"Heck no," replied Hank. "It expanded *my* business. Since Felix started advertisin', I never been busier!"

The men howled at Hank's joke, as Felix grew increasingly uncomfortable.

One of the men leaned forward and slapped Felix's shoulder. "Don't pay no attention to these guys, Felix. Better to go bankrupt at your age than mine. Your father can always bail you out!"

The man laughed, but a furious Felix didn't share his joke. "I'm not bankrupt," he said hotly. "Felix's Delivery is still in very healthy shape!"

One of the men threw a contemptuous look at Blackie, who stood very quietly, looking on. "Well, that horse of yours looks like he's on his last legs."

Felix began to seethe. He could put up with the men making fun of him, but when it came to Blackie he wasn't going to stand for it.

"Blackie is the best and smartest horse that ever lived! I just have to tell him where we're going and he goes." He glared at them all and walked away.

Hank Webster winked at Abner and followed Felix, calling to him.

"Felix! Come back here, boy!"

Felix turned slowly as Hank caught up with him.

"We're just giving you the pip, son! No hard feelings!" He smiled at Felix, his gold tooth glinting, his blue eyes twinkling. "Now listen. I have a little proposition for you. I got a contract to move some bags of sand from the train station to Markdale later today. Now, how about if I take half the load and you take the other half...and we'll see who gets to Markdale first? The winner will take the entire fee. How about that?"

Felix looked from Hank Webster to the group of expectant faces. He was torn. He wanted desperately to believe that these men were not simply humoring him, as Felicity had implied. After all, Hank Webster was treating him like an equal, man to man. But he knew, if he accepted the bet, he would be doing exactly what his father had forbidden him to do. On the other hand, if he said no, he would be admitting to these men that they were right. He and Blackie would be out of business...bankrupt. Besides, if he won the bet, it would certainly show Felicity, his father and everyone else that he could accomplish what he had set out to do.

"All right!" he said slowly. "All right! You're on!"

Felix and Hank shook hands.

"Okay, son," the older man said, smirking over his shoulder at the others.

Chapter Sixteen

Despite the briskness of the morning, Alec King wiped the sweat from his brow and put down the scythe he had been using to cut some of the long grass away from the root cellar in preparation for winter. He realized from his growling stomach that it was probably time to quit and have a bite to eat—if Janet would let him have a place at the table, he thought ruefully. His wife had continued to be fairly aloof at breakfast, even though it seemed the children had gotten over their quarrel. Good-natured Cecily, as usual, had decided to let bygones be bygones, and even Felix had been quite civil to Felicity. Janet worried too much, he thought to himself. Felix would come around.

He threw open the barn door and replaced the scythe on its hook, but the minute he turned to leave, he knew that something was missing. Felix's cart...it wasn't there. He strode across the barn to Blackie's stall. The horse wasn't there either.

"Felix!" he called. As he expected, there was no answer. His voice echoed in the emptiness of the barn.

"Oh Felix," he breathed, and he headed straight for Caesar's stall.

"All right, boy," he said softly, leading the golden horse out. "Here we go! Whoa! Don't worry...we won't take the buggy," Alec said as he grabbed a saddle and a blanket from the tack room.

Hank Webster whistled, cool and confident, as he headed along the road to Markdale. Left coughing in his dust was a very disgruntled Felix.

Hank, being stronger, had loaded his half of the sand into his buggy in jig time and had taken the lead immediately. Felix had caught up to him, though, soon after leaving the train station, but try as he might, he just couldn't figure out how to pass the man. The road simply wasn't wide enough.

"We'll never get by him," he complained to Blackie, who whinnied softly in agreement.

Halfway to Markdale, they were still in the rear, and the distance was widening between the two buggies. The situation was looking hopeless when Felix spotted an overgrown lane branching off from the main road. He recognized it as a short-cut he and Fred Bell had taken the previous spring to get to the Markdale Fair.

"I've had enough of this, Blackie," he said, pulling decisively on the reins. Blackie obediently turned off the main road and headed onto the path that led through the trees.

Caesar galloped full tilt onto the covered bridge, hooves clattering. Alec was barely able to hold him back from flying. If he had ever entertained any doubts about Caesar's background, they were forgotten now. It was all he could do to rein the horse in and stop at the blacksmith's shop, where Abner Jeffries was talking to a few of the men from the village.

"Abner! Have you seen Felix?" called Alec.

It was evident from their expressions that the men grouped around the fire could tell him something about the whereabouts of his son.

"He's racin' Hank Webster to Markdale...on a bet," replied Abner.

"He accepted a bet?" Alec couldn't believe his ears. The worst he had expected was that Felix had disobeyed his order to give up the business and was on another delivery. "When did he leave?" he demanded.

"They'd be halfway to Markdale by now, Alec," said Abner. "They left about a half hour ago..." He turned to the man beside him. "Wasn't it?"

"Give or take a few minutes..." replied the fellow, not quite able to look Alec King in the eye.

"And I suppose it never occurred to any one of you to try and stop Felix. He's only a boy! And Blackie's too old to be racing."

Alec shook his head in frustration, and giving Caesar a gentle nudge in the ribs, he rode away. The men looked at each other sheepishly and shrugged.

The winding road was much rougher and more overgrown than Felix had remembered it. The buggy lurched and bounced in the ruts that had been deepened by the fall rainstorms. Along the way, Felix had to shield himself from overhanging branches that threatened to scrape his face. The limbs of the trees almost met over the road, creating a cave-like feeling. Blackie steadily picked up speed, despite the heavy load of sand he was pulling. The wild scent of the woods seemed to spur him on, and Felix was delighted with the new energy the horse was showing.

"I'll bet we're way ahead of that Hank Webster by now, Blackie," shouted Felix. "We'll show him. We'll show everyone. They won't dare laugh at us again!"

As if in answer, Blackie pounded along the back road even faster. His canter turned into a rhythmic gallop. The trees passed Felix in a blur, and the cart bounced along as if it had a life of its own. "Atta boy, Blackie!" whooped Felix. Victory was at hand!

Alec and Caesar barreled along the main road to Markdale, but they had covered more than half the distance and there was still no sign of either Felix or Hank Webster. Alec had been following the clear markings of two horses and buggies until suddenly he realized there was only one visible. Backtracking, he saw that one set continued along the main road and another set veered off onto an overgrown lane. With very little urging, Caesar was more than happy to thunder off down the path through the trees

For the first time on the trip, Felix began to be frightened. Blackie was running as if the very devil was after him. Blackie had never run so fast in Felix's memory.

Branches and leaves whipped at Felix's face and he threw up his arm to protect himself. A cold sweat started to creep along his back, and he held his breath as horse and buggy careened towards a bend in the road that appeared just ahead of them. Suddenly, winning the bet wasn't as important as slowing his horse down. Felix pulled on the reins, yelling "Whoa!" as loud as he could, but Blackie ignored him.

The horse's hooves pounded and so did Felix's heart. They were never going to make the curve at this pace...not without tipping over. Felix held onto the reins for dear life, and pulling back on them as hard as he could, he tried in vain to bring Blackie to a canter, but the horse took the corner too quickly.

"Whoa! Blackie! Whoa! Whoa boy!" Felix screamed.

Behind him, the load of sand slid violently, and Felix felt the wheels on the right side of the buggy lift off the ground. They came down and connected with the gravel with a terrible bump. Felix's eyes widened. A bridge was suddenly looming ahead of them. Blackie desperately tried to correct his turn, but the momentum of the heavy buggy made it impossible for him to do it fast enough. They missed the bridge entirely.

Felix screamed as Blackie slid down the embankment beside the bridge and into the swiftly running water of a stream. The buggy followed on a steep angle, the sand in the wagon shifted forward violently, and Felix gripped the wooden sides in terror, trying to save himself from sliding off the seat.

Blackie finally came to a halt, but the weight of the sand and the momentum of the cart sent it slamming into the back of the horse. The next second, the cart hit a boulder on the embankment. The impact was tremendous. The cart twisted sickeningly, turned over and smashed. Felix felt himself flying forward, the bank of the stream a blur, the water coming straight for him. Rocks barely below the surface glistened darkly.

Alec galloped along the road, and a cold, foreboding feeling started to spread in the pit of his stomach. He knew instinctively that something was wrong. He urged Caesar on under the canopy of leaves, shielding them from a sky that had become a little too bright.

Felix opened his eyes, dazed. He didn't know how long he had been lying on the rocks in the stream. He sat up slowly, feeling dizzy and sick. He wiped the water out of his eyes and his fingers came away covered with blood. He stared at the red stain, not comprehending. Suddenly his eyes focused. The cart was broken. The water was rushing over it. The red paint of the lettering was running.

Sara's gonna be so mad, Felix found himself thinking. *After all her hard work*.

The stain spread on the surface of the stream... like blood. Felix felt his forehead again. More blood. He squinted, trying to focus. There was a great dark shape just across from him in the stream.

Felix struggled to his feet. A wave of panic rose in his throat. Blackie! He staggered over to the animal and frantically tried to get her to her feet.

"C'mon boy! Get up!" His own voice sounded far away, rasping.

The horse lay silent and still in the water. Felix pulled on her reins.

"C'mon boy! You have to get up! I'll give you a carrot! Blackie!" Felix shrieked the words, once again trying to pull the horse to her feet.

"Blackie! You've got to get up! C'mon! I'll help you." Felix pulled with all his strength on the bridle.

"Please Blackie! You've got to try! Just try! Blackie!"

"Felix!" came a faint call from the shore.

Coming upon the overturned cart, Alec had dismounted frantically from Caesar and scrambled down the embankment. For a moment he couldn't see Felix, only the wreckage floating in the shallow stream. Then, behind it, he saw his son.

Felix turned stricken eyes to Alec, blood trickling down his face. His father waded across the stream in two strides and gathered his son to him.

"Felix! You're bleeding!"

"He can't...he can't get up..." Felix cried, struggling and flailing in his father's arms.

Alec wrapped his coat around his son, but the boy fought it.

"I tried..." he gasped. "I tried..."

"Come on, Felix," said Alec, holding his son and guiding him to the bank of the stream. Out of the corner of his eye he saw Blackie in the water. Felix was fighting with all his remaining strength to reach the animal.

"No!" screamed Felix.

"Calm down," soothed his father.

Felix pushed him away. "No! You've got to help him!"

Alec turned slowly and looked at the still body lying in the stream among the rocks. He let go of Felix, waded over and stood above the horse. He looked back at Felix, whose eyes stared straight ahead, his teeth chattering from cold and shock. Alec waded back and threw Felix over his shoulder, carrying him over to the bank.

Felix hammered on his father's back with his fists. "No! No! Help him! Help Blackie! You've got to get him out!" he shrieked, half choking and sobbing.

"Calm down! Calm down, son. I will. I will," said Alec soothingly.

The sound of his father's strong voice penetrated through the shock, and Felix let himself be propped against the bank. Once again Alec wrapped his coat around the boy. Then, he turned and waded back out into the stream.

Blackie lay unmoving as the water lapped over her. Alec knelt and felt for a pulse. Again and again he tried. There was nothing. Slowly, Alec stood, his throat constricted, blinking back his own tears. He looked over at Felix on the riverbank, silent, shaking with cold, watching his father's every move. Alec slowly went back and sat next to him.

"Felix..." he began softly, trying to keep his voice steady. "Blackie didn't make it."

Felix stared straight ahead at the still body in the water.

"He didn't make it," his father repeated gently. "He's gone..."

A strangled cry tore from Felix's throat. "No!" Not Blackie! Not his friend!

Felix's body was racked with great choking sobs. Alec cradled him, rocking him gently as he cried in his father's arms.

Chapter Seventeen

Felix tore the company sign from his door and crumpled it in his hands. Then he went about his room, methodically and calmly getting rid of any mementos of his business. Without expression, he gathered up his business cards and leaflets and tossed them casually in a bin, along with the sign. Finally he turned his desk over and pushed it into its proper place, a dresser drawer once again.

A week had passed. His cut was healing nicely. A small bandage had replaced the larger one that Dr. Blair had applied the day of the accident. Felix had been confined to the bed in the kitchen for most of the week, but the minute he was allowed up, he had gone straight to his room. He looked around and nodded, satisfied that there was nothing left.

Later, in the kitchen, Felicity took a tray of steaming, golden-brown tarts from the oven, pushing an expectant Digger out of the way. Alec coaxed another mouthful of mashed carrots into Daniel, who waved his arms around, making it a very difficult task to feed him at all.

Janet glanced up anxiously from helping Felicity transfer the tarts to a cooling rack as Felix came down the back stairway and into the kitchen. He had disappeared up to his room hours ago, and she was relieved to see him. He hadn't been himself. She knew it was understandable, but she worried over his paleness and his withdrawn attitude. His bubbly, boyish personality had all but disappeared.

"Oh Felix! Come look!" Janet called to him in an overly bright voice.

"I've made your favorite," said Felicity. "Strawberry-rhubarb!"

Felix smiled good-naturedly. "No thanks! I've got chores to do!" he said jauntily, and grabbing his coat, he went outside with a little wave.

"I've got chores to do!" echoed Felicity in disbelief.

Janet and Alec exchanged worried glances. As soon as Alec put the last spoonful of food into Daniel's mouth, he rose from the table.

"When Felix can't wait to do his chores, something's up."

Alec lifted the baby from his chair and handed him to Felicity. He took his coat and headed outside to the barn.

Felicity looked at her mother. "Is Felix all right? He won't even let me in his room. He won't talk to me." Felicity had been filled with guilt since the accident. She couldn't forgive herself for saying the things she had to Felix, and she longed to make up for it in some way. Her mother patted her on the shoulder and stared out the window, watching Alec cross the yard.

The barn was quiet and still. Felix slowly crossed the floor and stared at the empty stall. Taking a deep breath, he went into it.

There, still hanging against the wall, was the special bridle with Blackie's name stitched on it by Cecily. He fingered it gently and buried his nose in it, breathing the smell of horse and leather deeply into his lungs.

Suddenly, the barn door slammed. Felix jumped at the sound, and then, whirling around, he grabbed a nearby broom and started madly sweeping up, as if he were simply doing his chores. He listened to Alec's footsteps coming towards him. He looked up and smiled at his father. Alec smiled back and walked towards the chicken coop.

"Oh! They're fine!" Felix called out to him. "I fed them. Boy, were those chickens glad to see me! I guess they were pretty hungry."

Alec listened quietly to his son. He was talking a little too fast and a little too much, his cheeks flushed and his eyes bright.

"Mind you," Felix went on, "they're laying a lot! I collected three dozen eggs! Three dozen! Can you believe that? I think it's some kind of record!"

Alec paused. "Can I give you a hand?" he asked.

"Oh! No thank you!" said Felix cheerily. "Just cleaning up! I'm fine!" He started sweeping with a vengeance, the dust and hay flying in the silence that had fallen between the two.

His father hesitated. "Felix?"

"What?" Felix responded without looking up.

Alec rubbed his hand across his face, trying to search for the right words...trying to express what he wanted to say in a way that Felix would understand.

"You know...my father...he believed that boys had to learn things the hard way, before they learned the right way."

Felix looked at his father quizzically as he struggled with the words. "But...I don't think... that anyone can learn the right way...unless they have some guidance. And...I should have given you more help."

Felix said nothing. He stared hard at the floor as his father continued.

"So, we both made some mistakes."

"It's all right," mumbled Felix. "Really."

Another silence fell between father and son.

"You sure I can't give you a hand?" asked Alec.

Felix shook his head. "No...I'm just finishing up."

"All right." Alec smiled uncertainly at him and turned to go.

Felix stopped sweeping and watched his father's back for a moment.

"You know that stuff you said," he began quietly.

Alec stopped and turned back towards his son.

"It wasn't your fault," said Felix, his smile growing crooked with the effort to keep his emotions in check. "I was responsible. I took the bet. I wish you just would have sold him. He'd still be alive..." His voice broke, and unbidden tears started to streak down his cheeks.

Alec walked to his son quickly and held him as Felix cried, leaning against his chest.

"Oh God, Felix," he said, stroking the boy's head, "I should have given you a little more help. I shouldn't have made you think I'd sell Blackie if the business failed. If I'd realized how much he meant to you, I'd never have sold him! And I'm sorry I made you feel you had to prove yourself."

Felix clung tightly, but he looked away, his eyes on the bridle hanging in the stall.

"But there are some things in this life, son, that you just have to put behind you," said Alec softly.

"I know. I will," replied Felix, gulping his tears away. "But...I loved Blackie. And I'll never forget him...ever..."

"I understand." Alec hugged him tighter.

"You go on," Felix said huskily. "I'll be out in a minute."

Alec stood back from his son and then, with a little salute, left him.

A shaft of light from the hayloft high above Felix suddenly felt warm on his face. He brushed away the last of his tears and walked slowly back to Blackie's stall.

Chapter Eighteen

"I...uh...just wanted you to know...I feel real bad about what happened..."

Hank Webster looked down at his boots, not knowing quite what to say. He twisted his hat in his hands, very uncomfortable under the cool scrutiny of Janet King. "It was a fool thing to have done..." he continued.

"Yes, it was," said Janet bluntly, shifting Daniel's weight in her arms. "But don't apologize to me."

She stared out to the paddock where Sara and Cecily were admiring his gift. Hank Webster had arrived a few minutes earlier, unexpectedly, and taken them all outside to greet his peace offering, a beautiful chestnut colt.

Felicity hung over the fence watching it, and so did Caesar, who had become instantly possessive of the new arrival.

It was a fine gesture, Janet thought to herself, but it was not going to bring Blackie back or restore her son's innocent joy of life. She was certainly not going to let the man off lightly.

Hank cleared his throat and bit his lip. He could see no forgiveness would be forthcoming from Janet, so when he spotted Alec coming across the yard from the barn, he hastened towards him.

"I'd like to talk to the boy, Alec," he said.

Alec looked the man up and down. Gone was the cockiness, the boasting, the taunting attitude. He was obviously sincere in his wish to make amends.

"Well, he's still pretty upset, Hank..." said Alec, looking towards the barn.

Felix appeared in the doorway. He hesitated when he saw Hank Webster, and then he glanced towards the paddock. The beautiful chestnut colt pranced in a circle as Sara led him by a bridle.

"He's so beautiful!" Sara's voice floated over to him.

Felix thought about his father's words. He still didn't know whether or not it was possible to put the things that had happened behind him, and in a part of his mind he knew already that he wouldn't entirely be able to, no matter how much time passed. Maybe that wasn't such a bad thing, either, he thought. He made up his mind and walked away from the barn towards the group.

Hank Webster smiled at Felix and shuffled over to greet him. "Hello, Felix," he said gruffly.

"Hello, Mr. Webster...Hank," added Felix, watching the man, his eyes slightly narrowed.

"I just want you to know that I feel real bad about your horse. I wanted to make it up to you somehow." He glanced towards the paddock and nodded in the direction of the colt. "His mother was a racehorse, just like Caesar."

Standing next to his wife, Alec winced.

"Felix," called Felicity, running over to her brother to drag him over to the paddock. "Come and see!"

Janet frowned as Hank Webster's words sank in. "A racehorse? Caesar is a racehorse?" she cried, and Alec and Felix exchanged pained glances.

"Since when have you been to the racetrack? Since when have you been betting on horses?" Janet demanded.

Felix decided to make a quick getaway and allowed Felicity to pull him over to where Cecily and Sara were patting the colt.

"Look how strong he is," said Sara. "He's the prettiest horse in Avonlea!"

Felix walked slowly to the fence. The colt immediately left Sara and Cecily's side and came up to him, staring somberly at Felix with great, sad brown eyes. Suddenly, it nudged Felix's pocket. Felix reached into it and, to his surprise, found a dried carrot, left over from...Felix pushed the thought away. Out of habit, he ate part of the carrot and gave the rest to the colt, who finished it hungrily. Tentatively, Felix reached out and stroked its soft muzzle, and the horse pushed against his pocket once again, looking for more treats.

"You're a hungry boy, aren't you, Star?" Cecily crooned.

"Star!" said Felix, with absolute disgust. "You can't call him a sissy name like Star!"

He took the horse's head between his hands and looked at him critically. "Your name should be ...Prince...or Conquistador...or Majestic Murphy! Like the horse we bet on in Summerside!"

"You took Felix to the racetrack too?" A horrified Janet turned to Alec. Then she stopped in mid-harangue and recognized the tone of her son's voice. The old Felix was back. A little older and hopefully a little wiser...but back.

She took a deep breath, and her frown melted into a smile. Alec knew with relief he had been forgiven, and he slipped his arm around his wife's shoulder and gave her a squeeze.

They watched together as Felix entered the corral. He put his face down to the colt and it nuzzled against him, still looking for food. Felix closed his eyes for a moment and saw a large, shiny black head instead of the small chestnut-colored one.

Again, memories and tears threatened to take over, but the colt made its insistent presence known. He buried his nose in Felix's pocket, then snorted with indignation upon finding it empty.

"Here, Felix," said Cecily quietly, handing her big brother an apple. "Do your trick."

After a moment's hesitation, Felix put the apple in his mouth. The colt gazed at him and took a few steps back, not quite understanding what the boy was up to.

"Come on! You can do it," Felix coaxed, talking with great difficulty past the apple in his mouth.

The colt approached, slowly and cautiously. He sniffed at the other side of the apple, backed away, sniffed again, and finally, to the cheers of his appreciative audience, took a tentative bite. That one taste was all he needed. His soft muzzle tickled Felix's chin and the apple was gone.

Suddenly, Felix was pushed from behind, and he turned to find Caesar demanding his fair share of the attention.

"It's all right, boy," said Felix. "We haven't forgotten about you." He reached up and stroked the animal's noble head, and Caesar whinnied with pleasure. Attracted by the sound, the colt came to Felix's side and nuzzled him expectantly once more.

A crisp breeze ruffled the colt's chestnut mane, and he pranced in one spot impatiently, staring deeply into the boy's eyes. As the first snowflakes of winter started to drift down upon the King farm, Felix took the colt's bridle in his hand and began to lead the new member of the King family around the paddock.

ॐ   ॐ   ॐ